SURVIVAL GUIDE TO
DATING YOUR BOSS

BY
FIONA McARTHUR

MILLS
BOON

First published in Great Britain 2011
by Mills & Boon, an imprint of Harlequin (UK) Limited,
Eton House, 18-24 Paradise Road, Richmond, Surrey TW9 1SR

© Fiona McArthur 2011

ISBN: 978 0 263 22090 2

Harlequin (UK) policy is to use papers that are natural, renewable and recyclable products and made from wood grown in sustainable forests. The logging and manufacturing process conform to the legal environmental regulations of the country of origin.

Printed and bound in Great Britain
by CPI Antony Rowe, Chippenham, Wiltshire

A mother to five sons, **Fiona McArthur** is an Australian midwife who loves to write. Medical™ Romance gives Fiona the scope to write about all the wonderful aspects of adventure, romance, medicine and midwifery that she feels so passionate about—as well as an excuse to travel! Now that her boys are older, Fiona and her husband, Ian, are off to meet new people, see new places, and have wonderful adventures. Fiona's website is at www.fionamcarthur.com

Also by Fiona McArthur:

HARRY ST CLAIR: ROGUE OR DOCTOR?
MIDWIFE, MOTHER…ITALIAN'S WIFE*
MIDWIFE IN THE FAMILY WAY*
THE MIDWIFE AND THE MILLIONAIRE
MIDWIFE IN A MILLION

Lyrebird Lake Maternity

CHAPTER ONE

TILLY loved Fridays. A leisurely walk down the hill from the hospital after her last shift before days off, that first salty sniff of the ocean at the end of Hill Street, and the bonus of Mrs Bennett, immaculately made up on her front porch as she waited for her girlfriends to arrive for Friday afternoon tea.

Tilly adored Mrs Bennett and her friends. Once famous sopranos in chic dresses, designer shoes and such lovely smiles, these ladies made Tilly believe in life getting better and better.

And they never mentioned men. She really liked that.

She couldn't wait to lift her window at the back of the house and hear the soaring notes of Verdi and Puccini from the porch at the back of Mrs Bennett's house—it always made her smile.

Tilly wondered if Mrs Bennett pulled her window shut when Tilly and her friends had their more rowdy parties.

Maybe she was strange to prefer the company of older ladies to boys her own age but risking your heart to a fickle man in the scramble to find 'the one' seemed much more insane to Tilly. Of course, she'd been a slow learner with *two* bad experiences in twelve months until Ruby had pointed out her 'pattern of disaster'.

Older men. She'd always been attracted by the big boys in senior school while she'd been a junior, then those in university while she'd been a senior, and now those who were out of their twenties when she'd just reached them. Searching for approval from the father she'd never known perhaps? That's what Ruby said.

Tilly sighed. Boys her age just seemed a little…insubstantial. She would just stay away from them completely.

The waft of real scones and Mrs B.'s Sydney Royal Easter Show winning marble cake dissipated the tendrils of regret and Tilly shook herself. It was Friday. Yay!

'Afternoon, Mrs B.,' Tilly called as she approached.

'Matilda. Lovely to see you.'

'Is that window sticking again?' Tilly drew level and Mrs Bennett smiled. 'No. I think you've cured it this time, dear. There's another one just starting to squeak and I'll let you know when it gets bad.'

More practice. Excellent. Tilly's last infatuation had been with a mature carpenter who'd turned out to be a secretly engaged control freak who liked to keep several women dancing off the end of his workman's belt. She was determined to never need his skills again. Just like the interior decorator who'd had so many rules and preferences on her behaviour and had then turned out to be married.

'No problem.' Tilly glanced up at the two bay windows, one each side of the veranda, and noted the one only a quarter pushed up. 'Girls coming soon?'

Mrs Bennett glanced at her watch. 'Any time now. I'll save you a scone.'

'Say hello for me.' Tilly swung open her gate and mounted the tiled steps. Home. And not a man in sight. Good.

Seventy-One Hill Street stood tall and thin with a decrepit Gothic air in need of even more TLC than Mrs Bennett's house.

Those tall eaves, all four bedrooms at the back upstairs and the main bedroom downstairs that belonged to the absent owner, could do with a good strip and paint. Tilly decided she might have a go in her holidays.

It was a real party house. The three other girls were the sisters Tilly had never had. She couldn't imagine life without their chaos and warmth and the fun they brought to out-of-work hours.

Tilly smiled to herself as she thought more about the girls. There was Ruby, a mental health nurse who didn't appear nearly as chaotic now she'd found Cort, a senior emergency registrar from the hospital they all worked at.

Tilly's need to provide a willing ear, and the occasional emergency alcohol, had decreased exponentially the longer Ruby and Cort had been together.

Ellie, an orphan, spent most of the week in sterile

operating theatres, but still managed to regularly fall in and out of love, searching for Mr Right to be the father of her longed-for family.

While Jess, children's nurse at Eastern Beaches, broke her heart every time Ruby's gorgeous brother, and incidentally their landlord, flew in from Operation New Faces with a willowy brunette or blonde on his arm.

Funny how her flatmates gave her plenty of scope for that thwarted older-sister tendency she could finally admit she had.

Then there was her job. Tilly ran up the stairs and threw her bag on the purple quilt cover on her bed. Tilly loved being a midwife.

Women were incredible, babies so instinctually amazing, and she could mother the mothers to her heart's content while they mothered their babies.

That's what she told Mrs Bennett later in the afternoon. They were clearing up after the girls had gone. Tilly's singing lessons by osmosis seemed to be working and she and Mrs Bennett were trilling away in the kitchen when the conversation came around to men.

'To sing that aria you need to be able to sing the love.' Mrs Bennett never joked about her music.

Tilly sighed. 'Then I'll probably never be good at it.'

'Of course you will.' Mrs Bennett's finger pointed skywards to the future. 'One day you'll find your man. You can't go on forever being single.'

Tilly laughed. 'You are. You're happy.'

Mrs Bennett twinkled. 'I'm certainly content. But

in a different way from when I was married to the love of my life.' She looked at Tilly. 'You can't miss out on that.'

Tilly shrugged. 'I always seem to go for the wrong guys. Seriously, I've nothing against men as friends but after the last two I guess I'm not really geared to be answerable to a man.'

Mrs Bennett fixed her with a stern look. 'They were too old for you, dear. And they lied.'

'You're right. That's what Ruby said. But look what falling for men does to my girlfriends. Even my mother was another casualty. I'm going to stay the sensible one cruising as a single woman for a few years. Travel the world. There's a lot I want to do and it's much less stressful.'

'Very wise,' said Mrs Bennett, and she smiled.

On Sunday morning, when Tilly caught a glimpse over the fence of a tall, black-haired stranger lurking around Mrs B.'s back window, her heart jumped at the recognition of danger.

She glanced back at her own house but the other girls were out and not due back for a while.

Her hand slid up to rest on her chest, ridiculous thought he'd hear her heartbeat, but for the moment it was up to her—someone had to protect Mrs Bennett.

Dry mouthed, she glanced around for a weapon, something, anything for protection, and then she saw it. Tilly's fingers closed around the pointed red beanie hat of the small but stalwart garden gnome at her feet and she eased him out from the damp earth under the hydrangea. The cold concrete sat heavily in her hand.

She chewed her lip. She really didn't want to maim the man, just slow him down a bit so he couldn't get away before the police arrived. With her other hand she flipped her phone and dialled emergency. At least she had a back-up plan.

Mrs B.'s ground-floor window screeched in protest and the material of the man's T-shirt stretched across his broad back as he tried to ease the window up quietly. A tall, well-built man should be throwing bricks on a truck for a living, not trying to rob defenceless old ladies. Tilly refused to be distracted by the tug of nervous suggestion that flight might be a better option than fight, judging by the ripple of musculature under the thin fabric.

He was trying to get into the house and Mrs Bennett was in there. Tilly felt a swell of pure rage surge with a helpful dose of adrenalin and she heaved the gnome with a straight-arm throw over the fence towards the backs of his legs. The gnome flew horizontally like an avenging angel and took out both backs of his knees in one blow.

Because the burglar had stretched up, his legs were locked and the muscles contracted with the blow.

Tilly stifled a nervous laugh when Goliath sat awkwardly back on the wet grass on top of the gnome and swore loudly.

Great job, Tilly congratulated the gnome, and backed back around the side of her house out of sight as she

flicked the damp earth off her hand. She couldn't help
the big grin on her face and the hormones rushed
around her body until she fanned her face with her
phone for relief.

The police call centre chattered and her hand froze
as she remembered. She brought the phone to her lips
and murmured quietly. 'Yes, I'm Matilda McPherson.
I'd like to report a burglar at 73 Hill Street, Coogee.
Mrs Bennett's backyard.'

'What the hell do you think you're doing? I'm fixing
the window, not breaking in.' Like an avenging archangel the man had found her and his dark blue eyes
blazed. 'I'm her nephew.'

He reached his long arm out, snatched the phone,
threw it on the ground and for one horrible moment
Tilly thought he was going to stamp on it.

Instead he drew an enormous breath, which incidentally did amazing things to the ripples under the front
of his T-shirt, and glared at her with the most virulent
disgust and even loathing.

Shame, that, a tiny, impressed voice whispered as
Tilly quaked just a little at his ferocity.

Now she could see his face it wasn't the face of a
criminal. He was very angry but he wasn't going to
physically assault her. She didn't know how she knew
that but despite Tilly's brain chanting 'Good time to
leave' in an insistent whisper, and despite the thumping
in her chest that agreed in rhythmic beat with her brain,
she couldn't allow him the satisfaction of thinking he
intimidated her.

Before she could say anything he ground out, 'I should sue you for assault.'

Yep. Daunting up close, especially with steam coming out of his ears, and Tilly blinked as she rallied. Maybe it was sensible to leave. 'Assault? A little woman like me? With a gnome?'

She tossed her hair to disguise the tensing of her muscles as she prepared to fly. 'Should look good in the local newspaper. Maybe they'll take your picture with the weapon?'

She watched with interest as his mouth thinned— might have been a better idea to keep her smart mouth closed—and then the moment when she was about to run was lost when Mrs Bennett poked her head over the low fence. 'Ah. Children, I see you've met.'

Mrs B. smiled beatifically as she came around the corner. She carried the gnome close to her chest and handed it gently, like a tiny baby, to Tilly.

'Look who came to visit at my house,' she said just as a siren began to wail in the distance.

Tilly glanced at the man's face. Apparently the siren just topped off his day.

By the time the police sergeant had laughed his way back to his patrol car Marcus was considering climbing back upstairs to his bed and pulling the lavender-scented sheets over his head to start the day again.

Instead he closed his eyes. Mainly because it removed the smart-mouthed redhead from his sight before he strangled her. From the fond look on his aunt's face the redhead was clearly a 'favourite person', and, to be fair, he supposed it was a good thing she looked out for Maurine.

'I am sorry.' The woman stood beside him on his aunt's veranda to see the policeman off. Didn't she have a home to go to?

He almost groaned. That's right. She did. And it was far too close to his at the moment.

To add insult to injury, she then said, 'Do your legs hurt?'

His lashes lifted only slightly as he glared at her. He forced the words past his teeth. 'I'm fine, thanks. If you'll excuse me.'

Marcus closed his eyes and sighed. If the rented flat fiasco hadn't happened, if the closest hotel hadn't been solidly booked for a week-long conference, if he didn't start work on Monday, if, if...

He ground his teeth and then decided it indicated a lack of control. Marcus liked control, relished it, had seen what could happen when it was lost, and he needed control to breathe.

He wasn't sure how he and his aunt would rub together, but if he remembered correctly from that one Christmas after his sister had died Aunt Maurine had been a safe haven in a sad world.

It would only be a week or two until he found a new flat. He'd buy one if he had to. Control. He rubbed his chin. Hmm. In fact, he liked that idea. Nobody could interfere with his plans then.

* * *

Tilly watched him go. Limping. Oops. She'd say that was a fair case of alienation there. Mentally she shrugged. Shame. He'd have made a gorgeous gene pool for Ellie's future children. Tall, good bone structure, great body, and even related to a delightful old lady. But he had no sense of humour. And that was the most important trait as far as Tilly was concerned.

Not that she was concerned. She frowned at herself. It had nothing to do with her how cleverly amusing Ellie's children could be.

Tilly went back inside her own house just as her flatmate Ruby arrived behind her, drifting up the stairs with a serene smile and a filmy scarf floating behind her.

'Hi, there, Tilly.' Ruby looked her up and down. 'You not ready? Sunday brunch at the pub?'

'I'd forgotten.' She glanced at the old grandfather clock in the corner. 'Give me ten.'

Twenty minutes later the girls were perched on stools looking out the Stat Bar window at the park full of football-kicking young bloods and the sea beyond. Another glorious blue-sky day in paradise.

Tilly weighed the words in her mind before she said them. She wasn't sure why she felt the need to curb her usual method of blurting stuff out. 'Mrs B. has a nephew.'

'Next door? Oh, my goodness, Tilly. That's so exciting.' Ellie sat blonde and beautiful and suddenly buoyant on the stool. 'Is he gorgeous? Does he like you? Would he like me?'

Tilly glanced at Ellie. Blonde, petite, beautiful. Who wouldn't? 'Not sure about you but he can't stand me. I took him out with a garden gnome.'

Three pairs of eyes swivelled to full interest. She certainly had their attention now, Tilly thought ruefully. 'I had the notion he was breaking into one of the windows at the back of Mrs B.'s. He was actually fixing it.' Tilly listened to herself, surprised at the glum note she hadn't expected, and injected more bravado. 'It was a good throw, though, sideways to the back of the legs.'

There was a stunned silence followed by a howl of amusement from the girls.

'What did he say?' From Ruby.

'Was he hurt?' From Ellie.

'What did Mrs Bennett say?' From Jess, who liked the older lady next door as much as Tilly did.

Tilly pulled the slice of lime out of the neck of her bottle of light beer and sucked it. 'He swore, he's got a limp, and Mrs B. got the giggles. So did the police officer who arrived.'

Ruby was impressed. 'You called the police as well?'

'I thought he was a burglar.'

'Very sensible.' Jess nodded. 'I doubt a real burglar would be happy with being hit by a gnome.'

'I'd bet he wasn't happy. What's his name, Till?' Ellie asked, clearly feeling sorry for her future partner.

'Marcus.' Tilly could see him in her mind as clear as day. 'He's six-four, blue eyes, dark curly hair and built like a brickie's labourer. Great genes.'

'Ohhhh.' Ellie's eyes shone.

'You sure you don't fancy him, Till?' Ruby was watching with those knowing eyes.

Tilly swallowed the rest of her beer and dropped the lime skin in. 'Not my type.'

Ruby and Jess exchanged amused glances. Ellie wasn't included because she was still off in dreamland, populating the world with miniature dark-haired brickies. 'Sounds like everyone's type to me,' Jess said.

'So how long's he staying?' That was Ruby.

'No idea. Conversation flagged after the police car drove off.' Tilly looked up and saw the laughter in her friend's eyes and she had to chuckle. Parts of the encounter had been funny. But the fact that he obviously hated her—would like to see her boiled in oil probably—wasn't amusing at all.

CHAPTER TWO

MONDAY morning sunshine streamed into the open bedroom window as Marcus towelled his shoulders. As he turned away from the streaky mirror he caught a glimpse of the purple bruises on the backs of his legs.

At least he wasn't limping today, no thanks to the red-headed witch next door. He hadn't gone for a run today just to give his legs a chance to heal. But he could have done with one to rid himself of the snatches of nightmares that had included dear Matilda. He didn't know why she'd made such an impression on him— apart from the physical imprint of assault.

He hung the towel evenly on the rail and walked naked into the bedroom. His aunt had been twinkling at him most of last night because it was all *so-o-o* funny. And he'd heard enough about Matilda with the legendary handywoman skills to make him dislike her even without the gnome.

But he wasn't wasting thought on annoyances because today was a big day. His mobile phone beeped twice, an appointment reminder that he had an hour until work, and as usual he was on time.

He'd worked hard for this. Not just the early stuff, sweating over a restaurant stove between uni classes, extra shifts right through his internship, and the study he'd put in for his O&G exams—it was the effort put in to give him the right to make policy changes.

To have a say.

To protect women and babies from idiots and poor outcomes and poor practitioners. An oath he'd sworn as a heartbroken child.

Now finally to be the consultant in charge of an obstetric unit, a small one by city standards but one with a brilliant reputation, and he knew exactly how he wanted it run. His mothers and babies would be the safest in Australia.

A snatch of song, a woman's voice drifting up from the garden below with a soft Irish melody that made the hairs prickle on the back of his neck. He lifted his head. The tune was pure and incredibly seductive and Marcus slung the towel around his hips and leaned out of the window.

His head whipped back in when he saw who it was. St Matilda in a bikini top with a towel around her waist. Long red hair crinkled wet from the sea like a siren's.

She was like a gnat, buzzing outside his conscious decision not to think about her, and he wanted to swat her. And that delicious backside of hers.

Whoa! Where had that come from? Heat descended

to his groin and he backed farther away from the window.

He'd been working so hard these past few years he hadn't had time for anything but brief flings. It was obviously just a physical need he should think about addressing again. Maybe he'd have time soon but certainly not in that neighbourly direction.

Plus she was too young for him. Though he had to admit just then he'd felt younger than he had in a while. He grinned then his leg twinged as he reached for his clothes and he thought of the gnome. Best to avoid the pain.

Two hours later Marcus surveyed his two residents, his registrar, and the MUM, Midwifery Unit Manager, in his new office as he outlined his plans. And it felt good.

They'd had a ward round on each floor, the gynae floor on top and antenatal beds next down with the antenatal clinic. Then the neonatal nursery floor and on the ground the birthing units and theatres.

He'd done a double take when Gina, the midwife in charge, had proudly pointed out the new large baths in the labour ward for pain relief in labour. Apparently they'd been put in from fundraising by one of the new graduate midwives but he hadn't commented as yet on that. No doubt she'd noticed her announcement hadn't been greeted with shouts of joy.

'Diligent observation with strict documentation, a medical officer for each birth if possible, though I do understand sometimes babies come in a rush. But I'd like admission foetal monitoring on all women until the baby's wellbeing has been proved. Risk assessment on every woman will be an area I'll scrutinise thoroughly.'

The medical officers all nodded, though Gina didn't look impressed. Well, tough. The buck stopped with him. 'Any questions?'

Gina spoke up. 'This isn't a training hospital for midwives. My girls are all qualified and very observant, up to date and extremely diligent already.'

'I'm sure they are.' But... 'Not all midwives have the same level of experience.'

Gina wasn't finished. 'I thought the studies said admission foetal monitoring increased a woman's risk of unnecessary intervention?'

He'd heard it before. 'I'm glad you asked that.' He knew what could go wrong. 'I've seen the studies but I'm not convinced. I'll leave some less publicised clinical trials for you to look at.'

When Tilly walked in for the afternoon shift handover there seemed an unusual quietness over the ward. There were a few gloomy faces from the students, the senior midwives were in a huddle with the MUM, and the other new grad, her friend Zoe, who'd almost finished her shift, drifted across.

'Why so glum?' Tilly looked at her with raised eyebrows.

'Dream's gone,' Zoe said sadly. 'Our new broom has arrived and we're not happy, Tilly. Ward meeting in five.'

Tilly frowned. At least she'd hear the worst instead of imagining it. They'd been so excited about the new consultant, too. With a younger man appointed to the post there'd been great hopes of a shift away from the medical model of over-monitoring and early intervention. How come the basic concept that women were designed to have babies had been lost somewhere in the teaching of new doctors?

Their previous consultant had been old school and a bit dithery, so you could almost understand his reluctance to change, but now it looked like they were worse off.

She followed Zoe into the meeting room. 'So he's not young and modern?'

Zoe pulled a face. 'He's young, majorly good-looking in a serious way, but not much of a sense of humour.'

Sounded like someone she'd met recently but this was not the time to think of social disasters. This was work and the thought of going backwards into a more medical mode of midwifery sucked big time.

Gina called them together and outlined the new directives. 'Full electronic monitoring of babies on admission for the moment, please, where possible. And he doesn't like the idea of the baths, but will tolerate them for pain relief as long as no babies are born in there, until we've reassessed the policy.'

Tilly couldn't believe it. 'After all our work? What's to assess? New South Wales Health said, "Make pain relief in water an option."'

Gina sighed. 'I hear you, Tilly. Just make sure your

women have been well informed, have signed consent, and agree to a land birth before they get in. We don't want that option of pain relief taken away until we can change his mind about the actual birth.'

That double-sucked. The last thing most women about to give birth wanted was to move, especially out of a warm, buoyant bath into a cool room and a hard bed.

Tilly chewed her lip and as the meeting broke up Gina drew her aside. 'This probably affects you most, Tilly. I know you put a lot of work into the fundraising. You have the same passion and instincts as your mother and all I can say is go slow.'

Tilly sighed and accepted she'd have to pull back. 'Doesn't sound like he'd appreciate Mum's philosophy.'

Gina smiled. 'Perhaps not that enlightened yet. We'll work on him.'

It didn't occur to Tilly not to grind her teeth. Control was overrated. 'It's offensive that we have to work on anybody. Back to being handmaidens. We should all be here for the women—including him.'

'Give him time.' Gina was always the voice of reason—a woman aware that passion needed nurturing and sometimes steering into less controversial paths. 'We'll show him we can provide safety and support as well as an optimal environment. Then he'll understand.'

The shift passed quietly, two normal births who arrived at the last minute, no time for excessive monitoring or to call for medical help, Tilly thought with satisfaction, and no sight of the new head of obstetrics.

Tilly went home consumed with curiosity and not a little disappointment. She wanted to see this man that had everyone quaking in their boots but she'd just have to wait.

The next morning, like most mornings since she'd moved into Hill Street, Tilly headed for the ocean. She couldn't help her glance up at the guest-bedroom windows in Mrs B.'s house.

Her dreams last night had been populated by a particular tall, dark and dark haired policeman who seemed to catch her speeding every time she drove onto a particular country road. No doubt there was something deep and meaningful in there somewhere but Tilly had been left with a feeling of anticipation and the wish that she actually owned a car to give her the chance of it coming true. Shame he wasn't younger than she was and she could try for a fling.

Maybe she should just paint the hallway. And refix the falling picture rail. That would keep her mind where it should be.

As Marcus jogged back up the hill after his run he saw three young women leave the house next door. The annoying one wasn't with them.

The crash and muffled scream happened as he passed her gate and the repeated swear word, not a bad one in the scheme of things, floated out the window towards him. He sighed.

Obviously she was alive, but his Hippocratic oath

demanded he at least check she wasn't about to do more damage. 'Hello?'

The swearing stopped.

He called out again. 'It's Marcus from next door. Just checking. You all right?' Marcus tilted his head and listened at her front door, which he could see was unlocked. Typical. Why'd she do that? Didn't she read the papers? Foolish woman.

'Um. I'm okay. Thanks.'

She didn't sound it. In fact, if he wasn't totally mistaken he had the feeling she was almost in tears. 'Can I come in?'

He heard the scrape of furniture and a muffled sob. Nothing else for it, he had to check.

'I'm coming in.'

She was sitting on the floor, the ladder was on its side and the annoying one was sitting beside it with her foot in her hand. He hoped to hell she hadn't fallen off the ladder.

He crouched down next to her. 'Matilda, isn't it?' As if he didn't remember. 'What happened? Did you hit your head?'

'Hello, Marcus.' She brushed a long tangled spiral of hair out of her eyes and his hand twitched at the unexpected desire to catch a tendril she'd missed. How did it spring all over like that and still be so soft?

'No. I wasn't up the ladder when it fell. But the hammer was. It landed on my toe.' She bit a decidedly wobbly lip.

He looked away, not because he wanted to gather her

up in his arms and comfort her, certainly not. He looked away to professionally assess her injury and saw one already bruising big toe. He glanced at her woebegone face then back at her toe.

Her gaze followed his. 'It throbs.'

'I imagine it would. I won't touch it until you get a bit of relief.' He glanced around the open room towards a doorway that looked like it led to the kitchen. 'Do you have any ice?'

She almost smiled and he almost melted. 'Always.'

He stood up. Quickly. 'I'll grab some from the freezer then.' Marcus stepped around the ladder and righted it before heading for the kitchen. He couldn't help a little peek around as he went. The house was very tidy.

He guessed that was one thing in her favour, though he supposed it could be any of the girls who had the clean fetish. He wasn't sure why he didn't want to stack up good things in Matilda's favour and refocussed on the task at hand.

Freezer. He saw the unopened bag of frozen peas and decided it would mould better around her foot. He grabbed a tea towel that was folded on the bench.

When he crouched back down beside her she looked more composed and he mentally sighed with relief. He mightn't have coped with her tears. 'I've brought the frozen peas. Less square.'

She took them and lowered them gingerly onto her bruised toe. They both winced. 'Ow-w…' she murmured as the green plastic bag settled around her foot.

'Where would you like to sit? Somewhere comfortable, maybe. With your leg up?' She couldn't stay there on the floor, which was cold tiles.

Her big green eyes, still shiny with unshed tears, so completely captured his attention he wasn't sure what she was talking about when she answered. 'Um...I'll try for the sofa.'

So far? So far so good? Sofa. Right. Move somewhere more comfortable. What the heck was wrong with him this morning? She lifted the ice and he helped her up and he saw her grit her teeth to take a step.

This was crazy. 'Here.' He picked her up easily in his arms and took the few strides to the three-seater lounge. She felt decidedly pleasant against his chest and it was with strange reluctance that he put her down.

Not sensible. He knelt down and looked quickly at her toe again as she prepared to replace the ice. The bruising was mainly below the start of the nail and he ran his finger along her slender, cute phalanges. He cleared his throat. 'I don't think anything's broken. Just bruised.'

She nodded then looked away from him and he suddenly realised he was still holding her foot. He almost dropped it in his haste to stand up. 'Well, if nothing else is hurt, I'll be on my way.' He unobtrusively wiped his hand on his trousers to rid himself of that warm and tingly feeling.

Big, solemn eyes looked up at him. 'Thanks for checking on me.'

The sooner he got out of here the better. 'My aunt would kill me if I didn't.'

She nodded. 'Of course. Thanks anyway.'

Marcus left. Quickly.

Tilly watched him go, her toe a dull throbbing ache that was being replaced by a dull throbbing ache from the cold peas, but the rest of her was still dazed from being picked up and carried as if she were a baby.

Scoop and go with no effort at all from him. It had been a very strange feeling to be held against that solid, manly chest and one she would have liked to have savoured for maybe a little while longer just for interest's sake.

Only to see why women liked it, of course. She almost got the reason. She could still smell the faint scent of virile man. Maybe guys did have some short-term advantages.

She glanced around at the flat-headed copper nails that had spilled out of the box and the hammer lying beside them. No more repairs this morning. Her toe was feeling better already and she'd be sensible to keep it up before work that afternoon.

She needed to remind herself that this guy qualified as an 'older man' and he pressed too many of her attraction buttons to be anywhere near safe as a platonic friend.

CHAPTER THREE

TILLY'S toe wasn't too bad by afternoon, probably that quick packet of peas, because she squeezed into her shoe with only a little tenderness before she caught the bus up the hill to work, rather than walk.

Tilly, along with the rest of the afternoon staff, had just finished their walk around the ward to meet the patients and for clinical handover when the phone rang.

Gina picked it up, listened, and then waved. 'There's a patient with foetal distress, first baby, coming in by ambulance.' Gina assessed the staff on duty. 'Home birth. Probable emergency Caesarean. You take her, Tilly.'

'Yep. Thanks.' Tilly felt the clutch of sympathy in her stomach and glanced at her watch. 'How far away?'

Gina looked at the wall clock. 'Ten minutes. Josie Meldon's the mum, from Randwick, and the midwife is Scottish Mary.'

Tilly was already moving. 'Who's the doctor on call?'

'The new consultant.'

So she'd get to meet the man. 'I'll page him and get the papers ready for Theatre.' More than anyone, Tilly understood the efficiency and reliability of home-birth midwives. And Mary was one of the best.

Tilly's mother and grandmother had both been heavily involved in the home-birth movement all their lives and Tilly had been born at home, naturally, as well as growing up holding placards at dozens of home-birth rallies.

She'd known Mary for years and if Mary said Caesarean, which she hated with a passion, that was what was needed.

She dialled the pager number for the new consultant then scooped a pile of preprepared theatre papers from the drawer on her way to the filing cabinet.

The cabinet held all the bookings of pregnant women in their catchment. Eastern Beaches Maternity Wing, or EB as it was known, had great rapport with the local independent midwives and in the last six months since Tilly had graduated she'd made extra efforts to liaise between the two areas of maternity care.

Tilly's goal had been to increase the mutual respect between hospital and private midwives, and while not missing, rapport hadn't flourished either.

Gina, a progressive manager and long-standing friend of Tilly's mother, had encouraged her. Now EB had brief admission papers of even the home-birth clients in case of emergencies such as this to streamline unexpected admissions. This benefited everybody, especially the incoming mums.

As Tilly lifted Josie Meldon's file the phone rang and Tilly picked it up. 'Maternity, Tilly. Can I help you?'

There was a brief pause and Tilly glanced at the light on the phone to check the caller was still on the line. Then a voice. 'Dr Bennett. You paged?'

'Yes.' She frowned at the fleeting illusion that she recognised the voice and then shrugged it off. 'We've a woman in need of emergency Caesarean coming in from home. Full-term baby. Foetal distress and her midwife is with her. I'm about to ring Theatre.'

'A failed home birth?'

The thinly veiled scepticism in the new doctor's response scratched against Tilly's nerves like a nail on a blackboard and she wouldn't have called the words back if she could have.

'Not really the time for labelling, do you think?'

He ignored that. 'She hasn't arrived for assessment yet? Hold the alert to Theatre until I assess her.'

Tilly frowned fiercely into the phone. 'That's your call but I'll still prepare the theatre notes.'

Another pause while he digested that and Tilly's flushed face glared at the phone. She wanted to get Theatre going.

'Who gave you permission to instigate a theatre call?'

'The midwife in charge of the case has called it. We're all working for the mother and baby, but just a moment,' she said sweetly, 'I'll put you onto the midwifery manager.'

Tilly held the phone with the tips of her fingers as if

she'd just discovered it was covered in horse manure. No wonder everyone detested this guy. She carried it at the end of a straight arm and handed it to Gina. 'I think this is for you.'

To Tilly's surprise Gina smiled wryly as if she'd seen this coming. Gina shooed her away to other preparations and Tilly gave no apologies for possibly upsetting the consultant. It was her job to help protect the women in her area. Thank goodness Gina knew that.

Marcus put the phone down after the brief discussion with Gina. He measured his steps to the door because what he really wanted to do was swoop down to birthing and shake his nemesis.

He couldn't believe the gnome thrower from next door was a midwife in his ward but he had no difficulty believing she'd champion home birth.

Home birth. The taste of it was metallic in his mouth, his least favourite association with his job, but even he could see that was personal and he shouldn't let it colour his judgement.

But he'd sort that after he assessed the new admission. 'Page my resident and registrar to meet me immediately on labour ward, please, Sheryl.' He spoke as he strode out the door and his new secretary nodded at his back. She was used to obstetricians in a hurry.

He briefly considered the shock he'd received when Matilda had been on the end of the phone. He tried not to think about the fact she would have told them all about the incident at his aunt's house. He was above out-of-school gossip and could ignore that the staff would snicker at the idea of him being hit by a gnome. And that he'd picked her up from the floor that morning.

Tough. He had more important things to think about.

The midwife in charge, thank goodness, was a sensible woman, but he wouldn't tolerate lack of respect from anyone, no matter how many windows she'd fixed for his aunt.

Marcus didn't wait for the lift and loped down the stairs two at a time, each step more forcible than the last, until he realised what he was doing. Calm. Control.

Tilly didn't give Dr Bennett another thought. She used a different phone to get a gurney over for her patient to transfer immediately to Theatre as soon as she had 'his' permission.

The ambulance arrived with her patient a minute later and Tilly directed them into the empty birthing room where she had the set-up for a catheter and IV ready to go.

Mary looked calm as usual but her hand shook slightly as she handed over her patient. 'This is Josie. We spoke about having a Caesarean on the way in, and that we'll have to put in a drip and catheter before surgery.' Mary's lilt was more pronounced with worry.

'Hi, Josie. I'm Tilly. One of the midwives here.' Tilly handed Mary the pre-jellied sensor from the electronic foetal monitor so they could all hear how Josie's baby's heart rate was.

The monitor picked up the clop-clop of the baby, a little faster than average rate but as soon as Josie started to get a contraction it slowed quite dramatically and

Tilly looked at Mary. 'I'll just pop the drip in while we wait for the obstetrician. Dr Bennett is our new consultant and he'll be taking over Josie's care while she's here.'

Tilly smiled sympathetically at the worried woman and her husband, and they all listened as Josie sighed heavily at the end of the contraction. When it was completely gone and her baby's heart rate had slowed even more they all waited with held breath until the rate slowly picked up and finally returned to the rapid rate of a compensating baby.

Okay, baby was coping and doing a good job of conserving energy, but not for long.

Tilly went on. 'It's rotten luck this has happened to you, but we'll try and keep you up to date as we go, and Mary and your husband can stay with you whatever happens.'

The door opened and a group of three doctors swarmed in like big white moths. Tilly didn't think it was fanciful to think they seemed to shrink the room.

The tallest moth was more like an avenging angel. An archangel she'd met before. 'I'm Dr Bennett. Fill me in, please.'

Mary stepped forward. 'I'm Josie's midwife.' That was all Tilly heard for the first frozen second or two because she was staring at the disaster that stood in front of her.

She felt like slapping her forehead. Dr Bennett. Mrs Bennett. Gnome man. This was a pearler. Wait till she told the girls at home. He didn't even look at her but somehow she knew he knew she was there.

Mary's voice drifted back in and Tilly listened distractedly as she went back to hanging the IV flask.

'Josie was doing beautifully, seven centimetres dilated, when we had a sudden dive of the fetal hearts with a good recovery the first time and then a repeat with a slower response.'

The chief white moth didn't say anything and Mary hurried on. 'Then the foetal tachycardia you can see on this graph. I'm not sure why, the response isn't dependent on position, but in case it was a true knot or something sinister we opted to come in. Each contraction has seen a slower recovery of the deceleration in heartbeat.'

'Of course.' His voice gave nothing away. 'What time did you notice the first deceleration?'

Mary glanced at her watch nervously. 'Maybe twenty minutes ago.'

He didn't say anything but inexcusable delay was the message everyone in the room heard. He looked away from Mary and his face softened into a reassuring smile as he leaned down and met Josie's eyes.

'You did the right thing, coming in.' He nodded and rested his hand on Josie's as she clutched the sheet. 'We'll have your baby out very quickly. Hang in there.' He glanced around at the rest of the people in the room. Tilly included. 'I want Josie on the table in ten minutes.'

Tilly felt the tiny slip of her leash and gave up on her silence. Didn't he have any idea how attuned Mary was to her women? She struggled, but thankfully her voice came out mildly, for her, as she gave in to defence. She waved the catheter in her hand. 'Thanks to Mary's pre-warning, the gurney's here and Josie's almost ready now, Doctor.'

His glance barely acknowledged her existence as he swept out.

'Holey dooley, thanks for the bat.' Mary caught Tilly's eyes and rolled them as she regathered her composure. 'Now I know what court feels like.'

'You do an amazing job, and have better statistics than a dozen hospitals, Mary. I don't mind telling people. He's new and doesn't understand but my manager says he's one of the best,' she said to Josie with a grin, 'and we'll have you there in under ten, Josie, so bear with us.'

Josie was in Theatre in eight minutes, once she was there a very quick spinal injection that numbed her took five, and her son was born ten minutes later.

Marcus peered over the green drape that separated Josie's upper chest from the operation site. 'A true knot in the cord, slowly pulling tighter as he descended the birth canal.'

At least he had the grace to nod at Mary, Tilly thought. 'You were right. Well done.' Then he looked back at Josie. 'A bit too dangerous for baby for a normal birth this time but he looks great now. He'll be with you in a sec.'

At the other end, waiting to take the baby, Tilly had to admit his technique was amazing. Swift, yet sure, and by far the most gentle Caesarean she'd seen since she'd started her training.

Sometimes the tugging at the end of the operation, that time as baby's head and body were removed after opening the uterus, could look almost brutal, but this baby had been scooped seamlessly and with a birth almost as serene as vaginal birth in water.

Tilly had to grin under her mask. No doubt another tussle she'd be having with this man.

Now that baby was safe, just waiting for his cord to be clamped and cut, Tilly could allow herself a little flutter of anticipation for the ongoing battle as she waited for Marcus to pass across their patient.

He looked calm. Calmer than he had when she'd taken him out with a gnome. Calmer than when the police car had rolled up. And to be fair, he'd been very calm and concerned and even kind when he'd come to her rescue that morning.

The surgical team had been quietly courteous and extremely efficient. The scrub sister was smiling her heart out at the pleasure of scrubbing in with him. And Tilly couldn't help notice his eyes glance Sister's way with a twinkle when she spoke. The silly woman was blushing over a smile and a few curling hairs at the V of his loose scrubs.

Marcus ignored the fact that he knew Matilda was watching him. He reached across and carefully laid Josie's baby on the sterile sheet on the resuscitation trolley and stepped away from the risk of contamination as she leaned forward.

It was Marcus's turn to watch. From the safety of his sterile field he watched the little boy wriggle on the sheet as she wiped him dry and murmured to him. It seemed she was good at her job. How annoying. He frowned at himself. That was ridiculous. That was a good thing.

He watched her as she assessed heart rate and breathing, along with colour and tone as she finished drying him.

Baby looked perfect, not distressed and she gathered him up with a deftness that spoke of experience and well-founded confidence. As she carried him around the screen to his mother, Matilda's pleasure shone and lit up the room. He glanced away because he'd almost smiled himself.

He saw the home-birth midwife's eyes mist as she sat beside Josie's head on the other side of the screen, not something he would normally have noticed, and he was left with a little disquiet at how abruptly he'd dealt with her. Hopefully he'd have a chance to reassure her before she left the hospital. Had he been insensitive? At least she'd known when to call it.

The next time he looked up it was because the little boy had begun to cry loudly as Tilly unwrapped him and draped him across his mother, baby chest to mother's breast, skin to skin. Tilly tucked one of his hands in under his mother's armpit and settled a warmed bunny rug over both of them.

He'd got over his shock and wasn't feeling quite as annoyed with her. But he'd have a word later. She was a militant little thing. He'd picked that up from the one comment she'd made in the birth suite. He should probably tell her he wasn't a fan of home births.

'Hello, my little darling. You scared us.'

Marcus heard the words as he began to suture the uterus back together. Such heartfelt relief, and he caught the moment when Josie's husband kissed his wife's cheek with a shuddering sigh. This was why he did this job. To keep families safe.

Half an hour later they were almost done. Baby had just let out a roar. 'Good set of lungs,' Marcus said as he looked over the top of the screen again and smiled warmly at the new parents, then his gaze skimmed Mary and settled on Tilly.

Tilly saw his eyes rest on her. We'll talk later, the look said. Now baby and mum were safe he appeared to be thinking of a little discussion about her phone manner perhaps. Good.

Tilly couldn't help the flutter under her rib cage, the flickering nervousness of a battle of wits and practice preferences, and she turned her head away from him. She looked forward to the challenge but perhaps it would be wise not to let him know.

On the return to the ward, Tilly sponged and settled Josie and her baby so Mary could go home much relieved. The rest of the ward was so busy Tilly didn't have a chance to wonder when Marcus would come to find her.

Which was just as well because he didn't get a chance that night, and apart from a few over-the-shoulder

glances that came up empty Tilly went home with unfinished business lying between them.

Marcus woke at dawn. He didn't know what had woken
him, but he knew it was hopeless to attempt further
sleep.

He rolled out of bed and stretched, seeing the sun
was tinging the horizon of ocean with pink and the
promise of another beautiful day. The lure of the salty
tang of a sea breeze had him swiftly change into his
trainers and let himself out of his aunt's house at a slow
run towards the beach.

A woman dived into the surf as he reached the sand
and he couldn't shed the ripple of anxiety as she disappeared under the waves. Her head popped up again and
he shuddered as old memories surfaced as well. Swimming hadn't been attractive since his sixth birthday.

Irresponsible, that's what it was, to swim so far out
and alone, he said to himself, then grimaced for sound-
ing like a grumpy old man. Well, for goodness' sake,
there were no others on the beach and the lifesavers
wouldn't start for another hour so who would help her
if she ran into trouble?

He turned his gaze to the sand in front and increased
his speed until the slap of his runners on the sand beneath him banished the memories and soothed his soul.

Out past the waves the woman swam parallel to the
beach from one side of the bay to the other and he sent
one brief glance her way as he turned to run up the cliff
path and onto the headland.

As he returned from his run he closed in on another girl, one he recognised, as she walked up the hill towards the house. One he'd meant to catch up with last night and hadn't had a chance to.

Unfinished work business lay between them but maybe that should keep for work. All he could think of was how amazing her wet siren's hair was, that wiggle of her walk under the towel wrapped around her that did uncomfortable things to his libido, and the strains of a haunting Irish lullaby, this time drifting backwards towards him.

Now, here was a dilemma.

He could run past and pretend he didn't recognise her and hope he made it into the house before she called out to him.

Or he could stop now, hang back, and not catch up.

Or he could fall in beside her and pretend he didn't care either way—which he tried but it didn't quite come off. 'Morning, Matilda.'

The lullaby abruptly ended and she glanced across at him. 'Good morning, Marcus. Or should I say Dr Bennett?'

'Only at work will be fine.'

Tilly grinned at him and he couldn't help his smile back. Not what he had intended at all. Neither was the slow and leisurely perusal of all she had on display above the towel. But what was a man to do when she looked so good?

She had the body of an angel, now that he had a chance to admire her up close, and the long line of her neck made his fingers itch with the impulse to follow the droplet of seawater that trickled enticingly down into the hollow between her perfect breasts.

Good Lord. His mouth dried and his mind went blank. Not a normal occurrence.

'Join me for breakfast?' He frowned. Now, why had he said that? It was the last thing he needed before work and gave the opposite impression of what he wanted to get clear between them. 'To discuss yesterday.'

She hesitated and he thought for a moment he'd get out of the ridiculous situation he'd created. Much more sensible to discuss work at work—like he'd decided before he'd been bowled out by his middle stump.

'Where?'

His stupid mind went blank again. 'Down at the beach? Pick somewhere to sit. I'll find you. Say fifteen minutes?'

'Something quick and light? Sounds good.'

A quick one. That's what he fancied all right and it was a damn nuisance his sleeping libido had decided to wake up when she'd gone past.

No. This was an opportunity to clear the air. About work. Maybe find some common ground on their perceptions of theatre calls and lines that were drawn. That was the sensible thing to discuss.

Fifteen minutes later theatre calls were the last thing Marcus wanted to discuss. She'd taken him at his word and waited for him by sitting on the steps of the white wrought-iron rotunda, a picturesque place of summer bands and vocal touters, and quite a fitting place for a mischievous midwife who drove him mad but a little public if anyone from the hospital walked past. He couldn't help glance around but nobody seemed particularly interested in them.

She *almost* wore an emerald sundress and up close the way it fitted her body took his breath and his brains away. Again.

He handed over the dish of fruit and yoghurt he'd chosen without thinking but thankfully she looked happy enough with his choice.

Then his mouth let him down. 'You look gorgeous.' He almost slapped his hand over it. *No-o-o-o.* Quick recovery needed. 'But I'm not a fan of home births.' The words hung starkly, like the family of swallows under the scalloped roof of the rotunda.

Her sudden smile faded. 'I noticed. Why?'

Good. She'd heard him. At least he'd said what he had to. 'Too dangerous. Poor outcomes if something goes wrong.' He looked away. 'And personal reasons. I really don't want to discuss it.'

To his surprise she nodded with more understanding than he'd expected. 'I can see that.' She glanced away to the waves.

When she said, 'Do you run most mornings?' ridiculous relief expanded inside him. He caught her eye as she looked back.

He could laugh now. 'When people don't cripple me with gnomes, yes.'

She bit her lip and blushed delightfully. 'I'm sorry. And I didn't mention it at work.'

He couldn't pretend that wasn't a bonus. Not the most glorious way to introduce the new consultant. 'I'm over it.' Actually, he was—surprising even himself—and Matilda looked happy to hear it. He let her have a full-blown smile so she could see he was telling the truth. 'I do have some sense of humour. Eventually.'

She looked down and smiled at the steps and he felt a frown on his forehead. Had he sounded self-indulgent? Forgotten how to talk trivia to a woman? Not usually. Maybe it was just this woman.

He forced himself on. 'So you like to swim in the mornings. And sing.' Her eyes lit up again, like they had in Theatre last night, and they smiled at each other like two loons. Then he remembered they worked together and he needed to keep distance. He glanced around at the people in the park. No one was looking.

There was an awkward silence and he patted the rotunda they sat on. 'Do you sit here often?'

She glanced around, encompassing the grass of the park, the sea, and finally the rotunda. 'When it's empty. I can see right out over the ocean. In the spring they have white daisies around the bottom. I pretend it's my castle and I'm a princess.'

Not too far-fetched even for his prosaic imagination. She looked like he'd always imagined a fairytale princess looked. He'd never had a thing for tiny blond-haired dolls, always dark, willowy Rapunzel-type ones, and red was close enough.

Problem was she so easily enmeshed him, like those nets hanging off the boats down on the beach, and he had to disentangle himself. A liaison with a junior mid-wife was the last thing he needed.

He just hadn't wanted misunderstandings at work and especially when his aunt thought so much of her. Really his only reason for being here.

He finished his breakfast in a hurry and stood up. 'Sorry to rush off.'

'No. You go. I'll stay a little longer. I often eat down here when I'm working the late shift.'

Tilly watched him go with his strong brown legs eating up the distance and the incline to his aunt's house. He didn't look back and his spine stayed straight and tall as he moved like a well-oiled machine, though actually he was a bit of a machine, with his running and his rules for the ward and the world. Marcus The Machine. A control freak. Which was sad.

Yet somehow she didn't think he'd planned the invitation to have breakfast with him. She smiled to herself. She'd bet that had come out of nowhere.

CHAPTER FOUR

WHEN Tilly walked into work that afternoon she didn't even get a handover. Gina shooed her straight through to Birthing as she arrived and briefed her on the way. 'There's a teenage mum in birth suite four. I'd like you to look after her.'

'Yes, please.' Tilly was happy with that and Gina grinned at her enthusiasm.

'India Ray. Her mum's in South Australia and the boyfriend's outside on the street at the moment. She has a nasty history of abuse and of course she's terrified of the birth and anyone touching her. The seniors will cover the ward until she's delivered so concentrate on her. She's had her monitoring done, so you can see the trace in the chart—all's well there.'

Tilly nodded, she could almost hear her mum's voice, 'If a girl's had a rotten childhood, past abuse can seriously affect the way she labours.' It had been a passion of her mother's that she'd passed on to Tilly, to be especially supportive and aware that labours could suddenly stop when women felt vulnerable. Privacy and actual physical contact were huge issues.

'Good luck.' Gina left her to finish handover with the others and Tilly knocked on the door and slipped into the darkened room. She could hear rapid breathing coming from the bed.

'Hello, there, India.' Tilly peered through the dimness and waited for her eyes to adjust. 'I'm Tilly. I'm the midwife looking after you this afternoon.'

There was no response from the young woman on the bed. Tilly tried again. 'How's it going?'

A sniff. 'My belly hurts.' India shot one agonised look at Tilly then stared back down at the sheet she'd drawn up to her chin as she lay on the bed curled up like a baby herself.

Tilly glanced around until she found the small mobile stool and her mind searched for ways to connect with the frightened young woman as she crossed to the stool. She sat, lowered the stool as far as it would go, and glided in at a much lower height than she'd been as she'd stood near the bed.

Her eyes were almost level with India's as the wheels stopped beside the clutched sheets.

She kept her voice quiet and conversational. 'It's hard work, this labour business. But worth it.' Tilly paused, in no hurry, letting India get used to her.

India grunted and Tilly bit her lip to stop a smile.

'Perhaps it's the bed.' As if the suggestion had just occurred to her. 'If you lie down with contractions they make your baby's weight crunch your back and hips. They say you feel the pain about ten times worse.'

India gritted her teeth. 'I don't want to move. I can't. And I hate needles.'

Tilly nodded. 'Sure. I understand.' She picked up the hand-held Doppler from the chest of drawers beside the bed and squeezed gel onto the end from the tube of conducting jelly. 'When you have the next contraction, can I listen to your baby, please? When we change staff for a labour we like to hear and say hello to your baby right at the start.'

She waited for India to nod that she understood.

The girl finally shifted her head slightly on the pillow in agreement and Tilly went on. 'After that I'd like to feel your tummy and the position your baby is lying in if that's okay with you?'

India shifted on the pillow again.

Not a lot of connection happening yet, Tilly thought ruefully. 'I could wait till after the next contraction for that bit, if you like, and then we'll see?'

Two thin shoulders shrugged under the sheet and Tilly smiled. 'Where's your boyfriend?'

'Outside. He won't stay with me.' India's lip quivered, 'Since I gave up smoking he smokes ten times more than he ever did. Today he's smoking a hundred times more.'

'That's hard. He'll be sorry tomorrow and feel rotten, though. Good on you for giving up. You need to keep healthy because this little person is going to keep you on the run.'

India defended her absent hero. 'Grant says he's trying to give up.'

Tilly held up her hands. 'No judgement from me. He'll quit one day then. Every time he tries to quit smoking he learns something that'll help him in the end.' Tilly nodded. 'Sounds like he's nervous and probably needs something to hold today.'

India glared at the empty doorway. 'He should hold my hand.'

'Yep.' Tilly looked down at the childlike hand clutching the sheet and felt a pull of sympathy. Support was so important in labour. She felt like nudging Grant wherever he was. 'He should.' Tilly glanced at the clock on the wall so she could watch the time between contractions and see how long it took until Grant came back. 'But when he's not here, if you need a hand you can use mine.'

Then she changed the subject so India didn't have to accept or decline the offer. 'Have you seen those cyber-cigarettes? They're rechargeable. Crazy. You use them like a real cigarette and they glow blue on the end when you breathe in. You even puff out smoke, but it's really just water vapour and nicotine replacement therapy.'

The first smile was always the hardest to draw but Tilly could feel the lessening of tension in the girl beside her when she finally smiled back.

'Do they work?' India was a very pretty girl when she didn't scowl. 'Sounds silly.'

Before they could follow up on that, a new contraction chased away any thought of humour as India hunkered down in the bed and screwed her eyes shut as the next wave rolled over her. Tears squeezed out beneath her clenched eyelids and Tilly slid one hand gently in next to India's fingers in case she wanted it.

Convulsively India's hand opened, grabbed Tilly's, and squeezed hard down on Tilly's fingers with her rings. Oops. She should have asked her to take the silver off first.

Tilly winced quietly until the contraction began to ease. 'I'm going to listen to your baby as the contraction ends now.' She extricated her blanched fingers and slid the little Doppler under the side of the sheet and onto India's round tummy.

The baby's heart rate echoed around the room in a galloping rhythm that made even India smile. The sound continued merrily as the contraction eased right away and after a minute more Tilly took the ultrasound monitor away.

'Baby sounds great.' Tilly wiped off the gel that was left behind on India's skin. 'Can I feel your tummy now, please?'

'Okay.' This time India looked more interested and Tilly smiled. 'Lovely tummy. Love your belly ring. Is that a little dragon?'

She nodded. 'My boyfriend wanted me to get a tattoo but someone said you shouldn't while you're pregnant.'

'Good choice. Not a great time to get an infection in your blood.' Tilly palpated the top of India's belly for the uterus with her hands and then the sides, and finally with both hands felt how deep into the pelvis

India's baby's head had descended. 'She's well down and pointing the right way. Looks like she's all ready to go.'

'How'd you know it's a girl?'

Tilly smiled. 'I don't. That's me being silly. I just call them all girls till someone corrects me. The other midwife said your mum is in South Australia?'

India brushed the hair out of her face. 'If she's still there. She's always doing a bolt.' India looked across at Tilly and her eyes narrowed. 'I'm going to be there for my baby no matter what.'

Tilly met her eyes and nodded. 'It sounds like you understand how important that is. Good on you. Is your dad around?'

'Is yours?' The answer shot back before Tilly realised she'd overstepped the boundaries.

'Sorry.' Word choice was so important. She owed India the truth because she'd expected it from her. 'No, not one who's there for me. I never even met him.'

She could almost see India's hackles subside. 'Neither have I.' And that was all they had time for before the next pain.

During the contraction India's boyfriend drifted in on a cloud of secondhand cigarette smoke and the room suddenly felt musty and sad.

India moaned noisily and Grant winced and picked up the remote control for the TV. 'Can't she have an epidural or something?'

Great support person, Tilly thought, but she didn't show any disapproval. Grant was all India had and less than perfect was better than none. 'We're thinking about a change of position first. I'm Tilly.'

After the introductions, Grant shrugged and then sat slumped in the chair and flicked the channels on the television. Tilly eyed the bathroom door with some hope.

'After the next pain how about you try the bath, India? The heat from the water and the weight off your back could be really helpful for the pain. You wouldn't have to have a drip in your arm like you would for the epidural if you decided on that.'

India's slim white shoulders shrugged. 'If you like.' She turned her head away and closed her eyes. Well, that was better than not wanting to move, Tilly thought, and went ahead to fill the bath and gather the towels before she went back to the bed.

'While we're waiting for the bath to fill, you could try standing up and leaning on the bed?' Tilly was nothing if not persistent. 'Just to get the weight off your back?'

India gave Tilly a long-suffering look that Tilly smiled at. 'Yeah, I know. I nag.'

Grudgingly India accepted the necessity. 'Guess you have to.' With much huffing and puffing, and no help from Grant, India was finally standing beside the bed.

The next pain came and she breathed noisily through it with a little more control. 'That was still terrible,' she said with a sideways glance at Tilly, 'but a bit easier to breathe with.'

Tilly smiled with satisfaction. Every little bit of

movement helped. 'Wait till you feel the water take all the weight off you and wrap you in a warm hug. It's worth the hassle of getting undressed.'

India's eyes widened with sudden comprehension and Tilly saw the girl's recoil at the thought of being naked. She was pretty sure Gina was right about past abuse. Tilly promised herself then and there she'd keep India safe and her privacy respected.

India didn't meet Tilly's eyes. 'I want to leave my top on.'

Tilly nodded enthusiastically. 'No problem. That's a great idea and you'll relax better. I'll give you a towel you can pull up in the water, too. It keeps you warm as well as covers you.'

India lowered her voice even more. 'If I had my baby in the water, nobody would see my bits.'

Tilly sighed. 'I know. And it's a great way to have a baby but at the moment we're not allowed to have the last moments of birth underwater. But you could be in there almost until the end.'

India scowled. 'Why not the birth?'

Yes, why not? Tilly thought mutinously, but kept her face bland. 'New doctor. New rules. But we can have the pain helped until the end at the moment.'

India looked sideways at Tilly. 'What if I don't get out?'

Tilly met her look. 'My head will roll and they might pull out the baths.'

'Oh.' India looked away

No more was said and Tilly acknowledged philosophically that India owed her no allegiance. So be it.

She was willing to take the consequences if it helped India realise her body was an amazing part of her and not something to be ashamed of. Tilly had a sudden vision of the look Marcus had sent her in Theatre yesterday and she'd bet a water birth would get more than a look. But maybe he'd get it if she explained.

Tilly helped the girl into the almost full bath and the dropping of tension from the young woman's face made everything worth it. 'Oh, my,' said India. She sighed blissfully. 'The bed was dumb.' India had power now.

Tilly couldn't help the pleased glow that made her smile. She loved this job. 'You can only do what feels right at the time.'

Tilly draped the towel over India's belly and legs and the water seeped into it quickly to create a warm, wet blanket over her bare skin.

'When you have the next contraction, towards the end of it can you lean a little over so that your belly comes up out of the water? I need to listen. It's good for baby to meet your germs but the fewer people who put their hands in your bath water the better,' Tilly explained. 'I still need to keep an ear out in case baby gets tired as we get closer to the end.'

India's eyes stayed closed and already she sounded more drowsy and relaxed. 'Okay.'

Tilly dimmed the lights. 'When you're ready to push, we can get you to stand up and have your baby. That way you can sit down again later.'

She heard a knock on the door into the main room and glanced down as India's eyes flew open at the noise.

India clutched the wet towel in a convulsive protective gesture.

They both watched the doorway widen to admit Marcus and his entourage until it seemed the room was full of men and Tilly sensed the tensing of India in the bath.

If she could just stall them long enough. 'I'll talk to them first,' she said quietly, and India nodded gratefully.

Before Tilly could say anything Marcus had seen her, absorbed the impending scenario, and already a frown crossed his face. There was no doubt he was unhappy with his patient in the bath. Or maybe any Tilly state of affairs.

His voice wasn't loud but it was definitely firm. 'I hope you're not thinking of a water birth in here?'

'No. Unfortunately not.' Tilly lowered her voice until he had to bend to catch her words, an unsubtle reminder that he'd still spoken too strongly for the quiet room.

More softly but with no less firmness he replied, 'Good.'

She stepped closer so she blocked out his assistants and the discussion continued between the two of them.

She used his comment to open for hers. 'Though the privacy and lack of contact would very much suit a frightened and self-conscious young woman.' She met his eyes and waited.

When he didn't say anything she said, 'I have no plan to flout ward policy and India's been told that we need her to stand up before the end of her labour. Would it be so bad if she did stay in the bath?'

'Yes.' His eyes bored into hers. 'I want her out before second stage starts, Sister.'

Now not even early second stage. Tilly chewed her lip. 'Such a shame when pushing in the bath would progress her labour more.'

His face tightened and Tilly knew she was skirting close to the edge. Obviously they'd already lost the rapport they'd shared that morning at the beach. Did she think they wouldn't?

It seemed two very different people faced each other now. She raised her brows. 'Is that the new policy? Out of the buoyant water at the beginning of pushing?'

They both knew it wasn't. Yet. 'If it's not, it will be.' They were both speaking very softly. It would have been funny if it hadn't been so serious. 'So tell me, Sister, how far dilated is my patient now?'

Tilly gave an infinitesimal shrug. 'Exactly, you mean?'

He raised his brows at her deliberate obtuseness and nodded. Like a terrier on a bone.

She shrugged again. 'I don't know. I'd say she's three-quarters of the way there. But as India's baby's heart rate is fine and she hasn't asked for pain relief, I haven't assessed her dilatation exactly.'

Marcus narrowed his gaze and the sudden coldness in his blue eyes drifted down her neck like a cool breeze. Uh-oh. Too far. It was him standing over her after the gnome all over again. Well, she hadn't run then and she wasn't running now.

He was seriously displeased and she wondered fleetingly what his problem was, but for the moment she was more concerned about her patient's problems.

He said, 'Shouldn't that information be available before entering the bath?'

Tilly only just prevented herself from rolling her eyes. Seriously. The guy had no idea. Water wasn't an invasive procedure. It was a heat pack. A drug-free heat pack.

Of course she couldn't not answer. 'Why? It isn't rocket science. A warm bath is a comfort measure that promotes relaxation, which helps progress in labour. Isn't that what we're after? Without drugs and side effects? Would you be happier with an epidural?'

'At least I'd know where she was up to.'

Tilly glanced back at the half-open door into the bathroom. 'My instinct tells me she's progressing rapidly now she's in the bath.' They were still whispering at each other and it must have looked strange to the other people in the room, though Grant was absorbed in the television and Marcus's residents continued to talk among themselves.

Tilly persisted. 'Unlike an uncomfortable vaginal examination, which only satisfies the curiosity of the caregiver and can change in a minute anyway.'

'And if something goes wrong and nobody has checked to find it?' Marcus was back to trying to contain that urge to strangle her again. Nemesis was right.

But he could do a war of whispers if that was what it took. And he would win. 'Please ask India to leave the bath and I would like an examination to indicate her progress.'

Then he let her know she was moving into dangerous waters in case she was as unaware as she appeared. 'I'm not happy with your attitude.'

'And I'm not happy with yours.' He really shouldn't have been surprised she'd said that. He'd watched her struggle to keep it under her breath. Pointless struggle.

The little witch. But a tiny part inside him had to admire her temerity, her dogged protection of her patient, but this was one fight he would win.

'Unfortunately I'm ultimately responsible for the safety of all the mothers and babies in my care.'

Still she wouldn't back down. 'And you think I'm not?'

Okay. Enough. 'We'll discuss this at another time.'

Her eyes gave it all away. 'I'll look forward to it.'

India's voice floated drowsily from the half-closed door into bathroom. 'Tilly?'

'Coming.' Tilly switched from combat mode to comfort. Maybe they'd wasted enough time to get what they wanted anyway. Tilly threw a glance over her shoulder at Marcus and closed her eyes briefly as she turned to her patient. She knew that tone. Not only were they going to have a baby in the bath, it was going to happen under the consultant's nose.

A tiny whisper from India that Tilly hoped didn't carry. 'I think it's coming. I can't move.'

'Get her out and onto the bed.' Marcus was behind her and when Tilly lifted the towel they could both see the time for moving was almost past.

If only he could see how easy and straightforward it all was, he'd have to change his mind. 'We're all here. It's safe. Can we just have the baby here, Doctor, then we'll move? Nice and calmly?' Tilly didn't pressure him. It was enough she'd asked. Just asked with a tiny hope he'd listen. It would be so much better for India in the privacy of the bathroom.

Marcus hesitated. 'It'd better be smooth.'

'I agree,' Tilly said as she knelt down beside the bath on the cushion. 'Just listen to your body, India. The doctor's here as well. Keep baby's head under the water until he's all out and then I'll help you lift him up and lay him on your tummy.' She looked around for India's boyfriend but he wasn't there. 'Do want me to call Grant?'

'No.' India shook her head vehemently. 'He doesn't like anything gross.'

Marcus heard it all. Watched Tilly settle herself. Suddenly he felt the familiar panic rise at the thought of a baby being born underwater, even though his brain told him it happened every day. Hundreds of them. If not thousands. But not under his very nose.

He couldn't believe this was happening. After all he'd done to avoid this very scenario. His head was telling him that babies had been born in water all over the world with no complications, some of his colleagues even encouraged it, but he hated it.

All he could see was his little sister floating face down in the pond. A picture that haunted him still. His fault. He should have seen she was missing. He'd sworn to protect her. What if this baby looked just like all those years ago.

He could still hear his own scream. He couldn't stand by and watch this. He turned and grabbed the towels Tilly had placed earlier.

'Pull the plug. Stand up, please, India. Now.' There was something in his voice that had Tilly scoop the plug and India rise to her feet before either of them thought about disagreeing.

'Now, step out and we'll get you to the bed.' His voice seemed strangely too calm as he wrapped the towel around the young girl's shoulders and between them they almost frogmarched her to the bed, where she climbed up awkwardly and sat back against the high pillows just in time for the birth of the head.

Marcus pulled on the gloves his resident handed him and he calmly cradled the rest of India's baby as she eased her out and up onto her mother's chest. Baby mewled like a kitten as Tilly dried her and India relaxed back into the bed with an incredulous gasp. 'My baby. That was so quick.'

It was all over in minutes, third stage complete, no damage, no problems, and a stunned India clutching her baby with a dazed look on her face. Tilly twitched the towel over India's waist to cover her lower half as Marcus stood back. Even Grant looked impressed.

'Congratulations, India,' Marcus said, and he still hadn't looked at Tilly. That had been so close. Too close.

As he left there was a tinge of irony only Tilly heard. 'I'll leave you in Sister's capable hands.'

Tilly fought to keep her face calm. He just didn't get it.

She forced a smile at a stunned India and Grant as they looked at their baby. India's face glowed as she stroked the little fingers that rested on her neck. 'Oh, my goodness,' India said, astounded she'd done it. 'It's over.'

'She's beautiful. And you are incredibly clever. You okay if I come back in a second?'

India nodded. 'Sure.' She smiled shyly at Tilly. 'Thank you so much.'

'You were fabulous. I'll be back.' She hurried after Marcus and shut the door to the birth suite behind her.

'Excuse me, Dr Bennett.' Her voice while quiet was anything but conciliatory and Marcus nodded at his residents to keep going.

When the young men were out of earshot he raised his brows. 'Yes?'

'That was bad,' she whispered. 'You got away with it but you've no idea how close you came to destroying her confidence.'

Marcus had assumed Matilda wouldn't like the loss of a water birth but he hadn't expected this. What was up her nose? He wasn't at all keen on her tone either. Young midwife Matilda was back to being a gnat.

He tightened the control. He wasn't going to lose

it. 'I'm sorry you think that.' His tone held a thread of steel. 'I see a well mother and baby with no ill effects.'

Tilly had her hands hovering near her hips, though she didn't go all the way and plant them. 'Did you also see a young woman with a history of child abuse sitting up on a bed with three strange men looking on?'

Marcus played back the scene. India hadn't seemed to mind at the time.

'If the birth hadn't been absolutely imminent so that she didn't have time to think of it, that exposure could have destroyed her.'

'I think you're over-dramatising this.'

'You burst into the bathroom and ordered her out of that bath like a bully. She didn't need to be on display on a bed. She could have just stood up in the bath.'

Marcus had never considered himself a bully, or been accused of it, and the idea was abhorrent to him. Despite the denial on his lips, he wondered if there was any truth to Tilly's angry accusation.

He hadn't known about the previous abuse. How could he? He'd evicted India from the bath for her own safety! Or had it really been for his own peace of mind? He shrugged all that off. It was something to think about later. For the moment this wasn't the time or the place. He wasn't happy being spoken to like this.

'That's enough. When you've cooled down we'll talk about this but not until you've recovered your temper.'

She glared at him and shook her head. 'If you'd thought more about the patient than your rules, you'd understand why I'm so upset!' Tilly spun on her heel and marched back to the birth room.

Marcus watched her go and then shook his own head. That was uncalled for. A certain midwife was in for a stern talking to in the privacy of his office. He used the stairs to go up to his office to get rid of the excess energy he suddenly had and arrived there much sooner than he'd have liked.

Tilly was on autopilot as she helped India enjoy that first hour after birth skin to skin with her baby and no interference as mother and babe bonded.

For India, Tilly knew it was important that she take her time and allowed Mia to find her own way to her mother's nipple, as Tilly had assured India she would. Thankfully, little Mia bobbed her way across her mum's chest and latched on by herself in under an hour. The less handling and help, the better India would feel about breastfeeding. Judging by the ecstatic smile on the new mum's face, and the sleepily replete blink of her daughter, India's life was about to change for the better.

Afterwards Tilly helped India shower and dress her baby, and even Grant seemed to turn over a new leaf and be supportive.

Two hours later mother and baby were asleep, tucked up in their respective beds side by side, and Grant had gone to celebrate.

The birthing suite stood clean and ready for the next arrival and Gina crooked her finger as Tilly put down the paperwork she'd just completed.

'Finished?'

Tilly nodded.

Gina smiled regretfully. 'Then Dr Bennett wants to see you in his office before he goes home, Tilly. Sailing a bit close to the wind, I fear, my dear.' Gina nodded, not unsympathetically, towards the lifts. 'Come and see me when you get back and we'll have a coffee.'

'Thanks, Gina.' Tilly stood up and squared her shoulders. Bring it on, she told herself, but the idea of putting anything in her stomach, let alone a coffee, wasn't a pleasant one.

She ignored the lift and trod lightly up the stairs to the consultants' rooms. Sheryl waved her to a seat and a minute later waved her through into the inner office.

She knocked and opened the door. Marcus stood with his back to her as he looked out the window.

'Please close the door,' he said without turning, his ramrod-straight back solid against the light, and Tilly felt the slow burn of irritation. Still, she did as she was asked.

Though if he didn't turn soon, she'd walk out. That sounded like a really good idea. 'Perhaps I'll come back later,' she said finally.

That shifted him. He turned and looked at her. 'Please sit down, Matilda.'

Nobody called her Matilda except Mrs Bennett and her mother when she'd done something wrong. Well, she hadn't done anything wrong except try to make her patient feel as comfortable as possible and she was blowed if she'd be raked over the coals for it.

Her chin went up and he didn't miss the moment. Typical. And dangerous. But she wouldn't care about that.

'Living precariously again? More will fall on you than a hammer on your toe.'

She lifted her chin higher. 'I don't know what you mean.'

'I'm in a quandary.' He gestured to the seat and he could see the reluctance as she sat. Trying to be fair, he sat, too, and studied her across his desk.

He fixed his eyes on her determined little chin, which was pointing so high he wondered if she could actually see him. That was part of his problem. She distracted him. Infuriated him. Made him lose the control he prided himself on, and he would allow no one, especially a little red-haired midwife with self-destructive tendencies, to ripple his hard-won equilibrium.

He'd never had this type of problem with a midwife before. A voice inside said he'd never been as dogmatic as he seemed to get with Tilly but it didn't really matter. He had to draw the line.

'You know why you're here. I need to reprimand you for disputing my orders, and in front of my assistants, and then taking me to task. That wasn't professional and I won't have a junior midwife tell me what to do.'

Her chin dropped a little and for a horrible moment there he thought it wobbled. He held his breath, suddenly terrified for a moment about what he'd do if she cried, but thankfully she didn't. But she didn't answer.

He couldn't help his voice softening a little. 'Do you agree?'

Finally she said, 'You had your own way in the end anyway.' He could hear the thickness in her voice.

He frowned. 'That's not the point.' That was too close. He'd actually wanted to stand up and pat her shoulder—or more.

But that would be weak.

Then she said, 'The point should be what's best for the patient.'

'Precisely. And I haven't seen enough medically based studies that prove water birth is as safe as land birth. I'm the one in charge.'

'I can show you studies.' It was as if she ignored the bit about him being in charge and his concern about her becoming upset dissolved rapidly. She was so annoying.

And still going on. 'I have well-documented hospital trials, though usually by midwives—because science isn't much involved. There's no uptake of drugs to measure just shortening of labour and lack of intervention. That's a bit harder to measure.'

He'd had enough. Protect him from zealots. 'I'll look into it more. In the meantime, I won't have any babies risked by birth underwater until we discuss it again.'

'Some rural hospitals have fifteen per cent of their births in water. I know of one that's over fifty per cent.'

'Matilda. Stop! I don't want that situation to arise again. Is that clear?'

She looked at him as if she'd suddenly remembered

where she was. She looked quite shocked actually and then put her head down. He wasn't sure he liked that.

'Yes, Doctor.' No apology but no defiance either. He could have said more. Could have cited worst-case scenarios, demanded a more detailed agreement. But he didn't. He needed this to end, too. 'Thank you, Sister.'

They both stood and she left with enough speed even for him.

Marcus sighed as he walked over and shut his door again. That hadn't gone quite how he'd planned and he wasn't sure he knew where it had gone wrong. Maybe it was because he could see that she was just as passionate about helping her patients as he was, only from the opposite side of the spectrum. He closed his eyes and massaged the stiffness in his neck. A damn shame the only fly in the ointment of his dream job lived next door and affected him like no other woman had before.

Tilly hit the stairwell at a run and she was halfway down before she slowed, sniffed, and thanked the universe she hadn't cried in front of him.

Why on earth had she felt like crying? Probably because she'd been mad. She'd been mad all right, thinking they could have a water birth in front of him when she'd been told it was off the agenda. But India had been so vulnerable and Tilly had wanted her to feel proud of what her body could do in her birth. It was only luck they'd got away with India not noticing the people in the room at the time.

She just hoped he didn't take it out on the rest of the

ward and ban the baths outright. Gina would be well within her rights to chastise her if that happened. She felt like slapping her forehead. What on earth had possessed her to push him so far?

CHAPTER FIVE

'AND then he just ordered me to pull the plug and India to move. When we could have had the baby easily in the bath.'

'Poor Till. But I bet you gave as good as you got.' Jess could be as militant as Tilly when it came to her passion for her own patients in the children's ward.

Tilly swallowed the tiny particle of guilt that tickled her throat. 'To top it off, I had to go to his office and get hauled over the coals as well later.'

It was midnight. All four girls sat around the kitchen table and sipped hot chocolate before they headed to bed.

'Didn't you say there's a no water-birth policy at the moment?' This from Ruby, usually the most alternate of them all. And that was not what Tilly wanted to hear.

'It's not in writing yet. And surely not when the birth was so imminent.'

'But he still got her to the bed in time?'

See what happened when Ruby fell in love with a doctor, Tilly thought mutinously. She changed sides.

Tilly knew that wasn't fair. Ruby had a point, but Marcus drove her crazy.

'Maybe something happened and he has a reason to hate water birth.' Ellie wasn't slow on the risks of this conversation deteriorating. 'Why don't you try and talk to him out of work time?'

Jess nodded. 'Yep. Good idea. Maybe drop in next door at his aunt's or maybe one morning? I think he runs—you might pass him one day.'

It felt strange to be on the receiving end of advice. She'd always been the one with the sympathetic ear. Tilly felt heat creep up her cheek. She'd never been a good pretender and didn't know why she hadn't wanted to mention the fact she'd had a little chat with Marcus this morning.

Before all this had happened.

Maybe because after the first brief mention they'd both avoided discussing the hospital, and what did that mean anyway?

'Tilly! You're blushing.' Three pairs of eyes swivelled to look at her and Tilly rolled her own at the inevitability of being caught out.

'I sort of had breakfast with him this morning.'

Now she really had their focus. To Tilly's relief, Ellie burst out laughing. 'With the father of my prospective children? Darn. I'll have to find another one now.'

They all laughed and Tilly relaxed. So silly, trying to hide such an event from her friends. 'It was just like you said. We met outside after his run and he asked me to breakfast.'

Ruby leaned forward. 'So how'd you get on? Did he flirt?'

Jess nudged with her elbow and a big grin. 'Did you?'

'Cut it out. It was fruit and yoghurt in the rotunda at the beach for a whole ten minutes. We talked about work and it cleared the air after that first disastrous time.'

But not the second.

She thought of the recent battle of wills, which had been a little too public for a junior midwife and the consultant. That might take more than Greek yoghurt and a light sea breeze.

Ruby laughed. 'So is he nice when you're not throwing gnomes at him?'

At least Jess was trying to keep her face straight. 'Has he any sense of humour?'

Of course he did. She didn't know why she was so sure about that when she'd been so doubtful. 'Well, he laughed a little about the gnome so that's a start. And he has a nice smile when it actually works. But I doubt we're friends after today.'

Ruby didn't agree. 'If he can forgive you a gnome he can forgive you a heated discussion. Besides, he didn't drag in the nurse manager, which he had every right to do. He dealt with you himself. I reckon that means he wants that episode finished and done and no leftover angst.'

Tilly thought about that. Maybe Ruby was right. She

didn't know how Marcus's mind worked. She wouldn't mind a bit more information on that mystery herself.

Something dark lingered over his view of water births and maybe one day she'd find out what it was. She'd gained so little insight into him but it was early days yet and she didn't want to know too much. She could guess where that would leave her. It was all very unsettling.

Ruby sighed and picked up her mobile. 'Well, as much as I'd like to delve deeper into Tilly's reasons for not telling us immediately that she had breakfast with the hunk next door, I have to go and soak in some beauty sleep for my own gorgeous man. I'm on the early shift tomorrow.'

Ruby turned back. 'But I think we should have a party this weekend and invite Marcus so we can all see what makes him tick.' She looked at Tilly. 'If you want him to come?' Ruby smiled at them all as she drifted away.

Jess yawned. Ellie unconsciously copied her and they both laughed.

'Party's a good idea. 'Night.' Jess gave Tilly a quick sympathetic hug and followed Ruby out of the sitting room and up the stairs towards her own room.

'Watch him, Tilly. Early days, though.' Ellie had the most experience of men and their foibles and knew how to bounce back. 'Take it slowly and look after yourself.'

Take what slowly? She'd just had an argument with the man. Been reprimanded. She wasn't looking for a relationship, not for years. It was unlikely there was any way she could have Marcus as a friend anyway, even out of work hours. Tilly rinsed her cup and switched out the light.

It was all very well for them. Ask Marcus to one of their parties? They were barely speaking to each other.

If she did ask him, it would definitely have to be a morning invitation and not done on the ward. He could only say no and she could live with that. Might be a whole lot easier if he did.

But what about her rule not to get involved with anybody? Still, she wasn't planning to get involved, it was just the possibility of an off-duty friendship that could be surprisingly pleasant. Nothing else.

Marcus saw the light go out next door as he lay with his hands behind his head and stared at the dark ceiling. He wondered which room was Tilly's and what it was like.

Then he squeezed his eyes shut for a second and dragged his mind away from next door and back to his own room. He could just make out the deeply sculpted cornices and the ceiling rose around the tiny chandelier above his head. He needed to get his own flat, somewhere away from here. Away from her.

Finally he fell asleep but his rest was anything but dreamless. Sleep gave way to another glorious sunrise, which helped banish the darkness of his latest dream.

He was six again. The house seemed full of people, talking in low voices, everyone busy as they fluttered around the bedroom, and those quiet moans his mother made that swirled in his tummy and made him feel sick.

Marcus wished this baby would just come out now but there was nothing he could do. He wanted to hold his mother's hand but nobody would let him near her. He couldn't do anything he wanted to do to make himself feel better. He had no choice in the matter. No control over anything.

'Your mother's fine.' His father gave him a quick pat on the head as he shooed him away from the bedroom door. 'Keep an eye on your sister, Marcus. I need you to be a big boy now.'

He didn't want to do that either. When the screams started he forgot all about Nell, could only put his little hands over his ears and close his eyes, until finally a faint baby's cry could be heard and everyone started to talk at once.

It was an hour later before he was able to see her. 'Where's Marcus and Nell?' he heard his mother ask in a weak voice, and he turned to the toy box, the last place he'd seen his sister.

Marcus shook himself and dressed quickly. The blue of the ocean reflected the cloudless sky and helped to dissipate the heaviness he'd woken with. Marcus sucked in a huge breath of salt-laden air when he hit the path outside and set off down the hill towards the beach.

This was good. The slap of his feet on the path, the freshness of an ocean breeze, and out in front an ocean liner crawling across the horizon with twinkling lights ablaze. Now, that was the last thing he'd ever consider doing—a cruise across a deep ocean. He shuddered and increased his speed.

The woman was swimming across the bay again and he suddenly realised it was Matilda. Of course it was. How on earth had he missed that yesterday? Risky behaviour was her bread and butter.

He couldn't get that picture of her wobbling chin out of his head. Which was ridiculous. He could understand if he was obsessed by her delectable breasts, but a chin? He really needed to get a grip. Get a grip. To his surprise a wide smile crossed his face.

An hour later he came up behind Matilda's towel-wrapped person as she walked up the beach and he couldn't deny his reaction was pleasure. Shame he wasn't some beach-dwelling surfer Joe with no issues and responsibilities. Maybe just for today he could pretend because he'd been pretty hard on her yesterday. 'Hello, there, Matilda.'

She stopped and turned his way, and to his relief she smiled at him without any hesitation. It seemed work stayed at work. He was ridiculously happy with that. She glanced behind herself and stepped back to sit on the sandstone wall that surrounded the beach. He followed her and they sat there and squinted back out at the waves.

'You really shouldn't swim so far out, you know.'

She looked at him quizzically and he knew he had no right to try to tell her what to do. 'And watch you don't fall off a cliff while you run,' she retorted.

'Touché.' They smiled at each other.

She hesitated and then fixed her gaze on his face

with a little of that jut of chin he could even become fond of. 'Actually, I should apologise about yesterday.'

Her cheeks went pink and he wanted to stop her. Let it all go, he thought, but she was right. His authority couldn't be questioned or it wouldn't work. He didn't say anything in case he ruined her effort at apologising but he genuinely admired her for bringing it up again.

'Anyway. I'll try to remember you're the boss.' She slanted a glance at him. 'At work anyway.'

To his surprise he laughed out loud. Not something he'd done a lot of lately and she joined him with a touch of relief. Was he that much of an ogre at work? The thought sat uncomfortably.

'Fair enough. Open season out of hours.' He changed the subject. That one had been done to death. 'So how was the water?' It looked cold and deep to him.

'Gorgeous.' Her eyes glowed and he thought the water wasn't the only thing that was gorgeous. 'I love it. Do you swim much?'

Not on your life. 'Not at all. Never learnt.'

She blinked at him and he felt like blinking at himself. Not something he usually volunteered.

'Then pleasure awaits you,' she said, and it pleased him she didn't utter the usual expression of disbelief.

'One day,' he said, and for the first time ever he wasn't one hundred per cent sure it wasn't true.

Absently she tucked damp hair behind her ear and he could feel his own fingers twitch with the urge to help. 'I've never tried to run for exercise,' she said. 'Too jarring on my knobbly knees.'

He glanced down, and the delightful length of really quite incredible legs made him think of anything but knobbly, but he teased her with a wise nod. 'I can see why.'

She flashed him a glance, saw the amusement in his face and burst out laughing. 'I wasn't fishing for a compliment.'

'I believe you.' He twisted to glance at the shops behind them. 'I thought I might try a fruit smoothie for breakfast to eat on Maurine's veranda this morning. Like me to order one for you?'

'Sure. I'll show you the best place for any type of crushed juice.' They crossed at the lights and walked past his usual breakfast place. He got the feeling she was trying to say something and he hoped it wasn't work related. He looked down at her but she was staring straight ahead.

'We're having a party on Friday night.' Now she looked at him as if relieved to get the first sentence out. 'Four of us live in the house. We all work at the hospital. You're welcome to come if you're free.'

Not what he'd expected but he didn't think so. He didn't do parties. Never had time. He'd be hopeless at it. 'I'll be tied up late Friday.' The words came out easier than the idea of attending. Plus it would be full of hospital people and he didn't want his friendship with Tilly to be a source of gossip. It would be easy for people to get the wrong idea.

Now he'd have to figure out where to go, though there was always plenty of work if he wanted it.

He realised Tilly had already moved on. 'No problem.' She shrugged and smiled at him and he wasn't sure what the feeling was he had now. Relief it wasn't a problem? It certainly wasn't disappointment that she didn't care. Was it?

'Come if you can.' She gestured with her hand at a fruit shop. 'This place here. They do the most amazing juice and smoothies.'

Ten minutes later they carried their drinks up the hill, and Marcus felt lighter and happier than he had for years. She was so relaxing. No pressure. Great to look at. Fun to be with. When not at work anyway.

He smiled to himself. Tilly didn't pressure him like other women had. She hadn't been worried at all that he'd declined her invitation. She was just a female friend and he couldn't ever remember having one of those.

Then his pager went off and with the noise he changed back into who he really was.

He lifted his phone and Tilly saw his expression change.

'See you later.' He took off and jogged the rest of the way to his house and disappeared inside.

Tilly sipped the creamy juice as she watched him go. With one phone call he'd looked like a battle-worn soldier going to fight. That was sad. For Tilly her work wasn't a battle: it was a watching game and a privilege. She guessed it was different for an obstetrician because they were called on when the chips were down. She wished she could show him how it should be.

CHAPTER SIX

IT WAS Friday night and Marcus heard the party as soon as he parked his car. He'd been trying not to think about it all day. No way was he going. He had a hundred reasons why he shouldn't.

There seemed to be an extra dozen cars, half on and half off the footpath up the street, and light and sound spilled out of the downstairs windows. He hoped it wouldn't go on all night. He wondered what his aunt said about this. It seemed pretty thoughtless. Bah humbug.

'Good grief, no, it doesn't bother me,' Aunt Maurine said with a laugh. 'I love the sound of the singing that comes later. And they put up with my girls on a Friday afternoon.'

She peered at him. 'You should go. Loosen up. You're a nice man, Marcus. I wouldn't like anyone to think you were a bit of a stuffed shirt.'

That straightened his shoulders. 'I'm not worried what they think.'

She glanced at him sympathetically and he didn't

like that either. 'And don't mind you haven't been given an invitation. The girls won't care if you just turn up.'

Marcus wrinkled his nose. 'I have an invitation, thank you.'

She raised suddenly haughty brows and he saw the lead soprano younger singers would have quaked at twenty years ago. 'Then why are you still here, talking to a woman twice your age?'

It seemed he had no choice. But he wasn't going like this in a shirt and tie. He'd stick out like a doctor surrounded by young nurses.

Ten minutes later he knocked on the door and discovered there were as many medicos as nurses dancing on the lounge-room floor and none of them cared.

He'd missed out on this at uni.

Always working, saving, studying. So this was what parties were like. It didn't look too wild. Noisy and colourful and someone had dug out a revolving colour strobe that painted everyone red and then green and then pink and back to red again. It was a wonder they weren't all having epileptic fits with the flashing lights.

Even the senior registrar from A and E he'd met yesterday, Cort someone, was there with his arm around an attractive redhead whom he thought perhaps lived here. It seemed he was right because she tilted her head back and called up the stairs.

'Tilly. Marcus is here.'

Then Matilda appeared. There was a big happy smile on her face and he could do nothing but smile back. She looked gorgeous again in black tights and a lime-green skirt with 1960s-style earrings that stroked her neck in the way he wanted to.

She drifted down the stairs like a debutante, slow and sinuous with a touch of shyness, and he held his breath until he realised what he was doing. He caught a sympathetic look from the A and E reg. but she looked too good to pretend he wasn't bowled over.

'I'm so glad you came,' she said loudly just as the music finished, and her voice fell into the silence. Everyone turned and looked at them both.

Marcus felt himself flush, and a shaft of regret and the wish he'd stayed home flashed through him for a moment, but then the music started again and she put out her hand and dragged him through to the kitchen where it was quieter.

'Sorry about that.' She even laughed and he realised she was unperturbed. Maybe he was a stuffed shirt but someone had to be responsible and he'd hate anyone to get the idea they were an item.

When he didn't answer she shook her head. 'It will be all over the hospital tomorrow.' She shrugged. 'Not a lot you can do about it. Just treat me like the annoying midwife you always do and you'll be fine. Everyone will think you're just slumming.'

She was teasing him again and he'd never realised she had a little dimple to the right of her mouth. He'd always known she'd had a mouth, a smart one. Tonight it was luscious and he had the sudden urge to taste her just a little.

He slipped his hand into hers where she'd dropped

it and pulled her in behind the edge of the refrigerator so that they were shielded from the door and he could back her up against the wall very gently but firmly until she was trapped.

By him. It felt remarkably good to have that power over her for a change. He put a hand on either side of her head against the wall, and they both knew she could duck under and out if she wanted to. But she didn't. Hmm.

'So,' he said softly and rubbed his cheek against hers. She felt like silk and no doubt he felt like sandpaper because he hadn't shaved since that morning, but she didn't seem to mind. If he wasn't mistaken, she almost purred.

'I like your perfume.' It was flowery and light and seemed to sing of summer.

'I like yours,' she said cheekily, and his smile widened.

He had another sniff and fought back the urge to crush her into his chest. He spoke to distract himself. 'It seems a good party.'

'All our parties are good.' And the way she looked at him said she had no problem with the standing arrangement they had at the moment. He felt his mouth tilt as he looked at her. Glorious skin, determined little chin, and that mouth. His eyes dropped.

He moved in until his chest flattened her breasts delightfully against him and she slid her arms up and around his shoulders. He liked the curl of her fingers against him and he pushed her earrings off her neck with his nose and brushed his lips along the line of her jaw like he'd hungered to do before. Her scent and the satin feel and the subtle pulse beneath his mouth felt more erotic than he'd expected.

Then their mouths touched, and joined, and he liked the taste of her even more. She made him feel like a parched traveller in a desert with a sense of homecoming and a caress of recognition. A taste of discovery and suddenly a taste of madness as they both learnt the other and found exactly what they'd never realised they'd looked for.

The perfect kiss, the perfect taste, the perfect fit and feel and depth, everything was right when it should have taken time to recognise and bond—yet instead they fitted together as if they'd waited for this moment.

Both pulled back at the same time, and if he wasn't mistaken, she was just as stunned and wary and not quite sure what had happened as he was. 'I'm sorry,' he said, 'I got carried away.'

The darkness of her pupils drew him. 'Funny. I thought there were two of us.'

Their gazes locked. He smiled. 'Were there?' They'd felt like one entity to him.

She laughed. It sounded a little nervous because this was moving too fast for an improbable relationship and at that moment the crowd surged through the kitchen door and into the room and they were surrounded by people looking for food and drinks. Tilly broke away, opened the fridge and began handing out platters.

Marcus leant back against the wall and watched her, and tried to figure out what had just happened.

Every now and then she cast him a quick glance, a shy smile, and he could see she was just as confused as he. He guessed that was something.

But he was strangely content just to watch her for the moment. The shift of her arms, the swing of her earrings against her neck, the pull of her shirt across her breasts.

When the crowds had been fed, he and Tilly moved back with them into the lounge, where the music had changed to a slower beat with a less deafening volume, and people lay around on cushions with at least two to an armchair and six along the floor, leaning back on the lounge he'd lifted her onto the other day.

'Give us a song, Tilly,' said a thin fellow Marcus recognised as the radiologist he'd spoken to earlier that day at the hospital, and a few more voices joined in.

Tilly shooed a young male nurse off her chair and pushed Marcus into it. Then she sat on his lap as if she did it every day and picked up a guitar from beside the chair.

He was trapped, pleasantly squashed, and wrapped in a surreal ambiance he'd never experienced before with this mystifying young woman and her friends. Suddenly he was a part of the crowd, instead of looking down on it, and it felt pretty good.

Tilly began to sing, quite unself-consciously, with that beautiful lilting ballad he'd heard before as she strummed the guitar. One of the male nurses joined in and within seconds a few more had joined.

Someone suggested a well-known song and suddenly the walls were bouncing with noise and laughter and Marcus looked around in wonder.

They sang a couple more and then people drifted out to refuel and recharge their drinks.

The sound system came back on and Tilly put the guitar down and leaned back against him, her face flushed and smiling. He kissed her neck. 'You're enjoying yourself?' He could see she was.

'Aren't you?' she said.

Actually, he was. Not a stuffed shirt at all. 'Very much. Thank you for asking me.'

A tiny smiled curved her lips and he wanted to kiss her again. 'It's not free. You have to sing. Your aunt has a glorious voice. You must have some inherited talent.'

He listened to a lot of music but he didn't sing. He didn't even sing in the shower or the car. But he wanted to please her. 'I could probably do a really mean "Poke Salad Annie".'

'Never heard of it.' She shrugged those delectable arms and his hand strayed up to curve over and cup the warmth of her shoulder. Her skin felt like satin beneath his fingers.

He sang 'Gator got your Grannie' in a Deep South baritone and she giggled. 'Oh, I like that. Do it some more.'

'That's enough, you two.' A pint-sized blonde grinned at them. 'Are we out of ice, Tilly?'

She nodded. 'I fear it's a tragedy.' She looked at Marcus. 'You're not drinking, are you?'

Not alcohol anyway. He was certainly imbibing something as she sat on him and he thanked goodness he had his shirt untucked. 'Nope. On call.' He patted his shirt pocket because he hadn't given his phone a thought in the last two hours. Thankfully it was still there.

She prepared to climb off him and parts of him mourned. She was oblivious, of course. 'Would you give me a lift to the pub and we'll get some ice, please?'

Ice sounded like a good idea, though he wasn't sure about dripping iced water in the tiny boot of his car. His mouth twitched. But he could think of worse things than having Tilly to himself in the close confines of his car in the dark. 'I guess I could. I'd been hoping to catch the submarine races anyway.'

She frowned. 'How do you see submarines race? Aren't they under the water?'

She was so naive. He liked that about her. 'Another name for parking in the dark. In a car with a girl.'

She slapped his hand away from her waist and stood up. 'There'll be none of that, sir.'

He tried to look crestfallen. 'Now, that's a shame. Do we get to put the ice in the refrigerator when we come back?'

He saw the moment she realised he was talking about the last time they'd been in the kitchen. Tilly looked at him from under her eyebrows and suddenly they were both laughing.

He captured her hand and dragged her out to his car. He felt like he was sixteen again, which was ridiculous when he was twice that age.

'So, you're enjoying your new job?' They were in the line-up of cars a few minues later to drive through the hotel bottle shop, and Tilly suddenly remembered the look on Marcus's face when his mobile had rung the other day. A soldier into battle.

He smiled at her. Tonight he looked a man happy with his world.

'Very much. And I enjoy private practice. It's satisfying to monitor a woman's progress through her pregnancy.' He drummed his fingers on the steering wheel. 'To know I've taken every precaution and been vigilant for the safe arrival of their precious baby.'

'Vigilant sounds like a force against evil.'

His hands tightened and she saw that his knuckles had whitened. 'Someone has to take the responsibility to ensure the safety of women and their families.'

Tilly mentally sighed. 'Okay, but healthy birthing women aren't at risk. You're not a control freak, are you?'

'What?' He didn't look happy with that.

Oops. She should have stopped there. Any progress they'd made tonight was about to go out the open window, and the warmth they generated between them cooled quickly when work became involved. Maybe that was a good thing if she was going to stay his friend and not anything else.

But, unfortunately, she couldn't stop. He was still

seeing birth as a battle. For most women it wasn't like that. 'Do you think perhaps you're treating pregnancy like an illness? As if a healthy mother is at risk for nine months and needs constant testing in case.'

'Probably.' His hands stilled and he glanced at her. 'Because some women do. It's a fact. Pregnancy increases risk. Things go wrong.'

She sighed. 'Sure. Some women need watching and expertise. But not all the time. Over-watching and interfering can draw bad outcomes, too. I guess what I'm trying to say is that normal pregnancy is not a disease.'

She saw the battle he was having with himself not to get heated and she felt sorry for him. They'd never agree on this and it wasn't fair to do this to him. She backed off.

'Anyway, I love watching the expectation as the due date appears. Meeting a woman's family, answering questions, and afterwards the glow of a new mother.'

She saw the relief he had something he could agree with or maybe it was just relief because the car in front had moved through and he'd be able to get out of the car away from her soon.

She'd done a good job of destroying their rapport anyway. Tilly rolled her neck in the dark. Dumb. Or deliberate subconscious sabotage?

CHAPTER SEVEN

THE morning after the party it was blowing a gale and the white caps on the sea were blown off the tops almost as fast as they formed. There were several strong rips dragging the foam on top of the water out to sea. On days like this Tilly opted for the women's pool for her swim.

Marcus ran past Tilly with a wave of his hand and she waved back. She was talking to a wizened old gentleman with faded blue swimmers emblazoned with 'Coogee Lifesaver' across his skinny buttocks.

The old bloke must have been swimming in the sea for seventy years at least, Marcus decided, or maybe eighty because his skin was as leathered and wrinkled as that of an anorexic sea lion.

The guy seemed to know Tilly well but, then, Tilly seemed to know everyone well.

Except him. He couldn't get a handle on her.

His feet slapped the sand as he crossed the beach and he reviewed last night in his mind.

He'd thought they were fine at the party but then

they'd gone for ice in his car, even though he hadn't been real keen to put wet bags in his car's boot. Tilly had seen his reluctance and teased him about it but he'd been brave about that.

He'd still been fazed by that kiss and the closeness of her on his lap in the lounge. He should have shut down that conversation about low-risk women earlier. Maybe kissed her to keep her quiet. That sounded much more fun. Her views on pregnancy and birth continued to jar him.

Soon after they'd arrived back he'd been called out and lost his chance to back her up against the wall again. Even now he could feel his body stir at the thought and he doubted he'd be able to look at a refrigerator in the same light ever again.

Before he could get to the top of the cliff path his phone rang and that was the end of his run. But that was okay. Diversion was a good thing. He turned round and jogged back to the house to get changed and go in to work on a Saturday.

The next morning they both reached the front path at the same time because he'd thought she might have slipped away yesterday to avoid him.

Tilly's brows drew together with mock suspicion and she looked up at him. 'Are you stalking me?'

He was trying hard not to but he'd actually missed talking to her yesterday. 'Could be.'

'Lovely,' she said, and they both smiled as they walked down to the beach. An easy silence sat comfortably on a sleepy Sunday morning. Even the waves were small against the beach now that the wind had died, and as they got closer the sun had already begun to warm the air.

'I was wondering if after our exercise you'd be interested in a long, leisurely Sunday breakfast.' There went his mouth again. It seemed he had it all worked out subconsciously. 'A table for two at the Beachside Bistro, browse the papers, enjoy the sun?'

She smiled at him and he was damned if he didn't feel like he'd just won a prize. 'Sounds wonderful.'

Excellent. 'Good,' he said out loud. He pulled his phone out of his pocket. 'I'll book a table by the window for eight.'

'Of course you will.' She shook her head and laughed at him. 'Leisurely, but with a timetable.' She reached up and kissed his mouth, a soft, promising kiss that almost had him flat on his back in the sand.

Then she patted his arm and left him where the path veered away from the water. He watched her drop her towel and then she was diving into the surf without a backward glance.

He stood there watching her as she swam and savoured the imprint of her sweet mouth against his. He almost wished he could dive in after her.

'Don't let her get away.' The old lifesaver from yesterday watched him with a quizzical lift of one snow-white eyebrow. 'She's a keeper, that one. Swim after her.'

'Love to.' He watched her lovely arms drive through the water. Then surprised himself again. 'Can't swim.'

The old man glanced at Tilly as she struck out through the surf until she reached the quieter waters of the bay. 'Then you'd better learn.'

In what spare moment of his day? 'I'm a bit old for arm floats,' Marcus joked, ready to move on.

'Six in the evenings. At the sea pool. I'm Duggie. Always there so it won't matter if you don't come. Might take a week or two. We'll see.'

The old man sniffed and moved on and Marcus stared after him. Good grief. He cast one last glance at Tilly then turned his face to the sand and began to run. He didn't want to think about the idea of putting his face in the water but thinking never hurt anyone.

An hour later Marcus's breakfast table was marked with a 'reserved' sign. Shielded by a palm in a window alcove perched above the beach, the table sat in the striped shade as the sun climbed up over their heads.

A tall black-eyed waiter placed a napkin across Tilly's lap with a familiar flick of his fingers and a wide smile. She laughed up at him. 'Were you scared I'd tuck it into my neck?'

The man raised one eyebrow and nodded. 'Absolutely,' he said, and Tilly laughed again.

Marcus thought it a bit strange, and a little intrusive for a waiter. 'Know him, do you?' He hoped so or he'd be having a word with someone.

'He used to go out with Ellie.' She glanced around

with a smile. 'Actually, most of these waiters used to go out with Ellie.'

Good grief. 'How many of them went out with you?' Now, why had he asked that? He certainly didn't want to know the answer.

'None.' She shrugged. 'I'm keeping it light. More of a looker than a participant. Burnt twice with ones who didn't work out. I'm saving up to do a study tour around the world in a year. Very happy being single.'

He raised his juice. 'Me, too. Here's to uncomplicated friendship.'

Tilly clinked her glass against his. 'Happy to have fun as long as it doesn't get serious.'

Perfect. An unexpected voice inside him wondered how much fun she'd agree to. Uncomplicated sex?

'I'll drink to that.' They both sipped as their eyes met and a smouldering frisson of awareness flickered across the table between them.

Tilly raised her eyebrows and smiled. He had to admit it was a strange conversation to have with a woman and laden with undertones. She dropped her eyes to the breakfast she'd chosen so far.

They started with tropical fruit and she licked her lips at the first taste of the most glorious cinnamon yoghurt. He'd had some before and he'd thought she'd like it.

'What is this? I have to find out.' She waved enthusiastically at her friend the waiter and the man came scurrying over with a big smile. It was almost as if she wanted to confirm she could flirt with other guys if she wanted to. No problem. Marcus tried not to frown, though he could have told her the brand.

He looked out through the windows and away from the two of them. The curving crescent of sand stretched both ways to the cliffs on either side of Coogee Beach.

He certainly understood why people thought Coogee was paradise. He could see the bay and other swimmers striking out like Tilly had across the blue water, then suddenly a flash of grey broke the surface.

'Look, dolphins.' He leaned forward and pointed and she craned her neck and upper body until she saw them.

Her breasts seemed to heave out of her top and he dragged his eyes away before she caught him looking but his good humour had been miraculously restored. The picture was imprinted indelibly on his brain and he'd pull it out and look at it again later. He grinned into his juice. 'Ever swum with dolphins?'

She sat back and it was safe to look again. 'Only once.' She smiled at the memory. 'They brushed against me and I nearly died of shock. Thought it was a shark.' She shuddered at the memory. 'But once I'd realised it was a dolphin, I remembered dolphins kept the sharks away so I felt better. I often see them a few waves away. Playing with each other. I know the day's going to be special when I see that happen.' She grinned at him. 'Dolphins mate for life, you know.'

Nobody mates for life. 'It's a lovely fairytale.' He returned to the previous subject. 'I can't imagine what you must have felt like when it brushed against you.'

He shook his head. 'I have enough trouble imagining the water underneath me let alone the sharks.' Marcus tapped his neck. 'If I was meant to swim, I'd have been born with gills.'

She disagreed. 'I was born to swim. I find it soothing to strike out through the waves. My mind wanders with the rhythm of breathing and using my arms and legs. It starts my day well.'

He could see that bit. 'That's how I feel about my run.'

She raised her brows. 'Don't tell me we have something in common?'

The rapport was back. And it felt good. 'I think perhaps we have a lot more in common than I thought—just a different way of looking at things.'

She gave him one of those smiles that felt like a precious gift. 'Marcus. That sounds very liberal for you.'

He grimaced. 'Let's not go there.' He stood up. 'Shall we try another course?'

The open buffet tempted them, and they piled their plates with mushrooms and tomato and a crispy rasher of bacon each. When Tilly saw they'd chosen almost identical breakfasts she laughed. 'Oh, no. An old couple with the same breakfast.'

'This once. Well-deserved appetite after our exercise,' Marcus said virtuously, and they carried their laden plates back to the seat with only mild guilt.

Back at the table they could see the dolphins were closer to shore and excited children pointed out to the waves. The sun was warm on his neck, the woman opposite was brown and gorgeous, and the sea and sand looked idyllic.

'I can see why my aunt loves it here,' Marcus said. 'I may have to change my plans of location if I decide to buy instead of rent.'

She nodded enthusiastically. 'Coogee has a great feel. It's young and vibrant, with a core group of great older people like your aunt and Duggie, and most of the houses and flats have so much character.'

'Duggie? The lifesaver. I spoke to him this morning.' He looked at her and remembered the kiss. He remembered it very well and it must have shown on his face because she blushed. 'He told me to dive in after you.'

She didn't meet his eyes. 'Duggie thinks everyone should be able to swim to Sydney Heads and back.'

Fat chance of that. 'He offered me swimming lessons.' That made her face him, he thought with satisfaction.

She zoned in on him with real attention. 'I could teach you.' Now he wished he hadn't mentioned it. What sort of man didn't swim?

She went on like a crusader and he didn't know how to stop her. 'I could. I used to teach the Nippers.'

Please change the subject. 'Nippers?'

'Junior lifesavers. Little ones. Most could swim but there were a few who weren't real happy about the surf.'

He could understand that. 'Sounds like me.'

Her face glowed and he couldn't tear his eyes away even though he wasn't happy about the reason for it.

'I love watching people learn to swim. I'm a good teacher.'

He could believe that but it wasn't happening. 'Not sure how I'd be as a student.'

She shrugged in that easy way that he really liked about her. 'If it doesn't happen, that's okay.'

Suddenly he was almost tempted. 'But time is against me.'

She sensed the opening he hadn't meant to give. 'If you got up a little earlier, we could do twenty minutes after your run.'

She was nothing if not focussed. Terrier-like. It was too much to ask. 'You'd have to get up earlier, too.'

She brushed that off. 'I'm a midwife. My kind got burned at the stake for doing what they love. Getting up earlier is nothing.'

Did he want to accept? He had a sudden vision of Tilly, in her bikini, directing his arms, and holding him to keep him afloat, lots of contact possibilities, much more fun than Duggie. 'I'll think about your generous offer. Maybe one lesson to try. I promise I won't burn you at the stake if it doesn't work.'

She grimaced. 'But happy to burn me for my mid-wifery.'

He looked down at his eggs. 'Pass.'

She raised her eyebrows and picked up her own fork and knife. 'Typical. Then pass the salt, please.'

The next day, back to reality on the ward round, Marcus hoped the time they'd spent together over the weekend wouldn't make it awkward at work—but she had said at the party he could treat her like the annoying midwife she was.

The thought made him smile. There was no doubt his little midwife did cause some measure of agitation in his manly chest and he was thinking of her more than he should. He'd really not planned to be distracted by anyone for a while but he had the feeling there wasn't a lot he could do about it now.

Tilly intrigued and amused him and turned him on with just a glimpse of her.

Later in the day he wasn't feeling quite so warm and fuzzy.

He'd gone down to the ward again to see his private patient, a woman who'd had a previous Caesarean because her induced labour had gone on too long, and now her second baby was due in two weeks.

Stella's repeat Caesarean operation had been arranged for the next day and he'd ordered a foetal monitoring session in the ward to check on her baby. Instead of a woman preparing for surgery he found that after an hour of exposure to Tilly, his patient had suddenly decided she'd like to cancel the operation, wait to go into labour naturally and try to have a vaginal birth.

Marcus suppressed a sigh. He'd had no idea Stella would prefer that. Had he missed something in their previous conversations or had Tilly swayed her?

He glanced at Tilly who looked back innocently. 'That's your right, of course, Stella,' he agreed. 'And, yes, it's true this baby may not be as big, although the ultrasound says a reasonable size.'

Stella peered at him as if to discern his own feelings about it all but that didn't help him figure out what she really wanted. He wasn't sure whether to blame Tilly or thank her.

Suddenly Stella burst into speech. 'If anything changed and I needed a Caesarean, would I still be able to have it?'

He tilted his head and frowned. It was a worry if he gave that impression. 'Of course you would. No problem. If you want to try a normal birth again, I'm with you all the way. Is that what you want?'

He didn't hold grudges with pregnant women. 'I thought you wanted the Caesarean because you were so exhausted from your last labour?' If that did happen again to her he'd quite happily strangle Tilly for encouraging her to go through a long first stage again.

'Tilly says if I go into labour naturally hormones are released that help my baby breathe better after birth. And Caesarean babies have a much greater risk of ending up in Neonatal Intensive Care.'

It was a risk they took every day but Caesareans were so common they didn't include that in pre-talks any more. 'That's all true.'

'You didn't mention that.' Her brows creased and Marcus kept his face neutral.

'I'm sorry. I thought you'd decided on the operative birth. I didn't want you to feel I was being negative about your choice.'

'Oh.' She looked a little shamefaced and he didn't want that either.

Sometimes pregnant women's emotions were a minefield but he got that. 'It's okay. Really. Whatever you want.'

In a less combative tone she said, 'So why do so many women have booked Caesareans?'

He really would have to spend more time with his ladies. It seemed it was too easy to assume they understood. He'd have to take that on board—it was just a little hard getting it from the junior midwife. Again. God bless Tilly. Not!

He looked at Tilly and raised his eyebrows. He hoped she could read the message. You started all this, his brows said, help me reassure her.

Tilly kept quiet. She probably thought she'd said enough, which he might agree or disagree with later, but for the moment he just continued because it seemed he had the stage.

Marcus pulled a chair over and sat down. His body language said he had all the time in the world to talk and Stella responded with a little drop of her shoulders. He focussed on her face, determined to ally her concerns. 'Because, as you said, operative deliveries have risk and we can't do all of our Caesareans in the middle of the night. It's safer when everyone is awake, full staff, and a mother hasn't any food in her tummy. That means booking them in advance.'

Stella frowned. 'Okay. But I might just go ahead and have a normal birth and not need an operation at all.'

He smiled at Stella. He really hoped she did. 'And I'll look forward to that.'

She chewed her lip. 'If I go overdue, can you induce me?'

Marcus shot a look at Tilly. Cat got your tongue? So you didn't tell her about that, he thought.

'Not usually. Because of your previous Caesarean it's better not to force the uterus to contract with drugs. Even with a natural progression of contractions you'll be closely monitored for any signs of the previous scar in your uterus coming apart.'

He hadn't spoken of that either, because he'd thought she wasn't going to have a labour.

'But we do have a special monitor that you can wear in the shower or walk around with,' Tilly offered, but Stella was on a roll with working herself up.

'Does that make my baby at more risk if I have a vaginal birth?'

Marcus shook his head. 'No. Only if your labour becomes complicated. You have no other risk factors. Baby's growing well, no medical problems. Statistically your baby is safer if born during normal birth.'

Stella nodded, satisfied, and smiled at them both. 'Then I'll go home and wait for that.'

'Fine.' He glanced at Tilly then back at Stella and dug in his pocket for his card. He wrote on the back. 'Here's my mobile number if you have any worries or more questions. I'll let Theatre know to cancel the case. It's honestly not a problem.'

'Thank you. I do feel better now. I'm going to do it

naturally.' Stella left, and Marcus waited for Tilly to come back from showing her out.

Tilly knew he was waiting and wanted to take a right turn and hide in the sluice room but she didn't. It wasn't her style.

'Um. Sorry she gave you the third degree.'

He raised his eyebrows. 'That was fun. Not.'

Tilly shrugged. 'She really had a lot of questions and once I started to answer them it just went on from there.'

He was partially to blame and that Stella might have been upset wasn't good enough. 'It's okay. I should have covered more in the rooms. But you were very quiet. I could have done with a bit more help to calm her down.'

He was right. Even to Tilly, her voice sounded sheepish. 'I thought I might have said enough.'

She looked relieved when he half laughed as he turned to go. 'Probably.'

'Are we still swimming tomorrow?'

He glanced at her with wide eyes. 'Am I going to have to do it naturally?'

It was Tuesday morning.

'Let your body float. Trust the water. We're designed to float.' It was seven in the morning and the first of the lessons with Tilly. 'The water's not even up to your waist and you can stand up any time.'

She definitely had a thing about trusting water. They were poles apart.

Sitting in this position, the water was up to his

nipples. It was cold and very salty. Funny, he'd never tasted the salt in sea water before 6:00 p.m. last night.

Thank goodness he'd come and at least become a little more comfortable in the water. Duggie had been very matter-of-fact about his reluctance and this morning he could sit in it without shuddering. No way had he been going to make the first attempt in front of Tilly.

But he didn't know if he really wanted to do this. Thank goodness there wasn't anyone else around. 'This is ridiculous.'

Tilly's voice was in his ear. Comforting. 'Just lean back on me, Marcus. I've got you. If anyone sees us they'll just think we're having a cuddle.'

That was the only reason he was still there. Tilly's skin against his in the water, satin with an underlying strength, and the softness of her breasts against the back of his head. It could certainly be agreeably erotic if he wasn't so unhappy about the water and the chance of people looking at them.

Her hands were around his chest loosely as he leaned back and she shifted farther away as he stretched out. He wouldn't have minded rolling the back of his head around that lovely cleft but she might drop him. He snuggled a little with an internal smile. She never lost contact. He knew she was there. Reliable.

Her voice went on. Warm and wonderful and he could see how she helped women in labour. 'Close your eyes and just feel it. Spread your arms out. Let yourself relax and I'll hold your shoulders.' He closed his eyes. Actually, it was better with his eyes closed. Like a cold bath. Suddenly he could feel his weight shift and his legs lifted as he stretched right out. He was floating!

His eyes flew open and he stiffened, and as he sank water nearly ran into his mouth. He gasped just as Tilly's arms came around him and kept him above water level again.

'Nearly.'

This was pathetic. He made himself sick with this stupid fear. Something shifted in his mind and he forced himself to trust her this time as he leaned back against her. This time he relaxed his body into the sand on the bottom of the sea pool.

His legs drifted towards the surface and he fought the urge to stiffen. His head leaned back more as she shifted away, still with her hand under his shoulder blades but that was all.

His ears submerged and then he was floating. He kept his eyes shut and pointed his toes until he stretched out fully. She had the tips of her fingers under the back of his head but he was doing it all himself. It wasn't too bad.

When he sat up and looked at her with a grin—darn it, he was pleased with himself—she grinned back. Even more delighted than he was. 'Okay. You're a good teacher.'

Her eyes opened wide, innocently green. 'That wasn't what you said when Stella changed her mind about the Caesarean.'

Cheeky. 'Ouch. Nasty woman. I'll remember that next time at work.'

'Ouch, yourself.'

Fifteen minutes later they were walking back to Hill Street. 'What are you scared of, Tilly?'

Tilly shot a look at him. 'What makes you think I'm scared of anything?' She flicked a stray hair out of her eyes. 'Apart from trusting men, of course.'

He laughed. 'Can't help you with that one. But seriously?'

I was serious, Tilly thought. 'Um. Suturing?'

She saw his incredulous look. 'Suturing?'

What was so bizarre about that? 'Yep. I did the suturing module and passed but I'm a terrible seamstress with real sewing and I'd hate to do a botched job on a lady who's just given birth.'

He pursed his lips. 'Fair enough. So we could practise that. I learnt on foam. Then we could do steak. Neat little stitches. I'll teach you on the weekend. Then I'll feel I'm repaying you for the swimming lessons.'

'There's no debt, Marcus.'

Maybe she didn't see one. 'I'd like to do it.'

She tilted her head. 'I think I have issues when you're nice to me.' Then she smiled at him and it ran down his body like a bolt of liquid heat. 'Okay. Thanks. But not till before lunch. I have something on during Saturday morning.'

He nodded. Satisfied. 'Brunch at your house. I'll bring supplies.'

She paused at her gate. 'We'll have a barbeque after

with our carpetbag steak.' They grinned at each other. 'Ruby's a vegetarian. She'll hold her nose when she smells the meat.'

CHAPTER EIGHT

THEY managed to get through the rest of the week without any major confrontations at work, and even some
sweet moments during births, when he tried to be as
unobtrusive as possible and observe rather than direct.
He'd had a few memorable smiles from Tilly.

By Saturday morning, after his swim, he was looking forward to brunch. There seemed to be some type
of rally going on and it was pretty noisy. The beach park
was full of baby strollers, toddlers, militant mamas,
doting dads and purple-dressed women whom Marcus
finally realised were home-birth midwives. He could
feel his lip curl.

Placards abounded. 'Home birth is a choice.' 'Babies
birth naturally.' 'Midwives hold the future.'

Marcus rolled his eyes. He'd gone for his run late because he'd been up half the night with a tricky delivery
and subsequent emergency Caesarean. All had turned
out well but it had been touch and go for a while there
for mother and baby and his eyes felt like sandpaper.

Imagine if that woman had been at home. These were

exactly the sort of people his parents had hung around with. Hard as it had been to accept after his sister's accidental drowning, he'd never really come to terms with any parents' decision to have their baby's birth outside the hospital in a non-structured environment.

'A well mother and baby can be safer at home than in a hospital. Leave medical care for sick mothers and babies.' The words penetrated his heated thoughts and he froze. He knew that voice.

'Midwifery care is safe care. Everyone wants well mothers and babies. Tell your local member of parliament that you want the choice of safe home birth.' Why was he surprised? But he wondered if the hospital allowed their midwives to promote such dangerous practice.

He tilted his neck past the dreadlocked hair in front and now he could see her. Dressed in a purple sundress, her height raising her face slightly above those on the old-fashioned park bandstand, the gazebo they'd sat and had breakfast together in, as she gazed earnestly out over the sea of faces.

He pulled his head back behind the woman in front in case she saw him. There was a smattering of applause and nodding heads as she left the dais.

He felt let down, back-stabbed, incredibly hurt—which was ridiculous. He'd known she was passionate about natural birth. But he hadn't known she was a radical.

He put his head down and turned away but it was

slow moving through the suddenly dissipating throng of onlookers.

'Marcus?' Tilly touched his hand and he straightened but he couldn't look at her. He stared into the distance where an oil tanker was crossing the ocean out on the horizon past her left ear.

His voice was flat when the words came out. 'You're part of the home-birth movement, aren't you?'

She straightened her shoulders. He saw the shift, but couldn't look at her while he waited for her to confirm it. He didn't want to see the truth. Just watch the damn ship crawl across the waves, he told himself.

'Yes, I am. Absolutely.' Straight up. No flinching. Of course she was.

He looked then. Stared straight into her eyes. Said goodbye to her eyes, her nose, that mouth. The features he'd come to like a lot. Not love, it couldn't possibly be love, but definitely feel attached to. But whatever they had between them was over. Had to be because she stood for everything he distrusted.

'Well, I disagree with all of it. And I'd rather not become involved with someone who is. I'd consider it professionally hypocritical.'

Her fine brows were raised and for the second time since he'd known her she was angry. 'Spending a little time together doesn't make us involved. But I'd hate to make you a hypocrite, Marcus.' A lot of irony accompanied that comment.

Her emotion practically singed his eyebrows as her eyes bored into his. 'You're a big one for generalisations, aren't you? Why are you so closed off and negative about something that should be every woman's right?'

Why? Did she have an hour? 'Because it's dangerous. Because people die or almost die.' Now he was angry at himself for making it personal.

He saw her face change. Soften instantly at whatever had crossed his face but he didn't want her sympathy. She said, 'I'm guessing something happened.'

'That's not important.' He wanted her to understand he could never encourage a birth at home for one of his clients.

'To me it is. Can't you tell me?' Caring eyes looked into his and he didn't want that connection.

And he really didn't want to remember that day. He'd been six and his baby sister had drowned. That's why he'd never learnt to swim, but he didn't say it. He looked past her to the ship that was almost gone. 'Nothing happened. Goodbye, Tilly.'

He'd go to his consulting rooms and put the whole thing from his mind. There was plenty to do there. He could do that. Because he had control.

She watched him walk away with his shoulders straight and his head up but she knew how much he was hurting. She'd wanted to tell him that the unexpected happened in hospitals, too.

That home birth had evolved and midwives were trained, skilled, updated more than ever before. Professional women doing a professional job. And women at risk were share-cared with a doctor when they should be. But he was gone and she had a lot to think about.

She guessed there was no suturing lesson this morn-ing or carpetbag steak.

When she went home his car wasn't there. Mrs Bennett was sitting on her front veranda, drinking a cup of tea.

'Hello, Matilda,' she called, before Tilly turned into her own gate. 'Fancy a cup of tea?'

Tilly stopped and went up the path in Mrs Bennett's and joined her on the veranda. She glanced at the little table beside Mrs Bennett's knees. 'And scones? Yum.'

'There's plenty in the pot. I thought Marcus was joining me but he's torn off somewhere in that car of his.'

Tilly wondered if she was the reason he'd 'torn' off. 'It must be nice to have him here for company.'

'Yes. It is.' Mrs Bennett poured for Tilly. 'Strange, when I'm used to my own company, but nice. He's a good man and easy to live with. It was lovely to see him go over to your party the other night. I don't think Marcus's done much of that sort of thing. Takes things a bit seriously, I think. He used to be such a happy little thing. Singing made-up songs all the time until the tragedy.'

Tilly couldn't help the soar of interest those words provided. 'Did he?' This was sneaky but no way was she leaving. She settled into her seat.

Mrs Bennett nodded. 'His mother almost died during a birth at home. Not something a child should watch. Silly woman. She had a bleeding disorder, never told the midwife or they wouldn't have allowed it, and should never have had the babe at home.'

Home-birth horror story. She should have known. 'He never said.'

'You might need to give him a bit of leeway if he seems serious. I don't mind telling you, Matilda, that boy was hard done by. His parents didn't make enough effort to make him see it wasn't his fault.'

'How could his mother's birth problems be his fault?'

'Not his mother's. His little sister died the same day. There should have been other adults there looking after those children while his mother birthed, not putting a six-year-old in charge of a three-year-old.'

Tilly felt the cold clutch her belly. Water, she'd bet. 'Poor Marcus.'

'Of course the boy was too young to be responsible with all the screaming that I'll bet went on. His little sister wandered away and drowned in the fish pond they had out the back.' Mrs Bennett bit her lip and wiped away a tear.

Now she'd upset her friend. Tilly felt terrible. 'I'm sorry if talking about this made you sad, Mrs Bennett.'

Mrs Bennett sat up straighter, pulled one of her immaculately ironed lace handkerchiefs out of her pocket and dabbed her eyes. 'It was a very sad time. But I don't mind tears. Might be the actress in me.' She gave a watery smile.

'Tears always make you feel better, that's their job.'

She sniffed delicately. 'They were all so airy-fairy in those days. Flower children twenty years after the movement finished.' She snorted. 'Well, they nearly lost two flowers that day by not being responsible and poor Marcus was saddled with the guilt.'

Tilly could see a solemn little Marcus bowed under the horror of that day. How devastating. She wanted to pick him up and hug him. No wonder he was so serious sometimes.

'Anyway...' Mrs Bennett straightened in her chair. 'He worked his way through uni the hard way, deter-mined not to ask for anything from his parents. Not that they ever saved a penny in their lives, despite being very intelligent people. Not practical, you know. Luckily Marcus was very independent even then.' She sighed. 'Still, he turned out well.'

Except for control tendencies, mistrust of women, and an aversion to water. Tilly picked up her cup. And she'd bet he'd be horrified his aunt had shared that with her, not that she'd break that confidence. Tilly hoped Mrs B. wasn't trying to set them up together because they were just too different.

When Tilly went next door an hour later she certainly had a lot to think about.

Ellie was setting the table and she looked up when Tilly entered. 'What's happening with you and Marcus? Thought he was coming back today for suturing les-sons?'

'Not today. We've agreed to differ. Again.'

Ellie studied Tilly's face. 'That's a shame. I actually felt you could suit each other.'

Tilly turned away. 'I thought you wanted him for his genes.'

Ellie grinned. 'Plenty more fish in the sea.' She looked down at the plates on the table. 'Which reminds me, Jess gave up on your barbeque. She's bringing fish and chips. Should be back any minute.'

Tilly groaned and held her stomach. 'Mrs B.'s been filling me up with scones. Small plate for me.'

After four days of avoiding Tilly, late one afternoon Marcus dried his back and grinned at Duggie. 'I can swim.'

'Not a bad stroke.' The old lifesaver was standing on the beach beside the lifesaving shed after their lesson.

Marcus nodded and allowed the concept to sink in. He should have done this years ago. 'Yep. It's not pretty but it works.' And he was happy with that, too. He could do a slow, solid freestyle that was anything but flashy, and it had come out of nowhere and didn't tire him at all.

It seemed that Tilly, along with Duggie's pithy help, had conquered his fear well and truly.

He studied the ocean in front of them and out to where a man was swimming across the bay, and he thought of Tilly again. Something he did with monotonous regularity despite telling himself to stop. 'But I'd hate to have to rely on my own steam to save someone out there.'

Duggie nodded. 'Best not to try without something

to help you float. Gotta have a plan. But get one quick because people do drown.'

He followed Marcus's glance. 'Always think what you're going to do when you get there. You don't fight with the ocean. Or the person you want to help.' He pointed to a young man battling through the waves on his way out to catch a wave on his board.

'See that!' He shook his grizzled head. 'He's got his head up, he's daring the waves to slam into him. If he stayed low on the board, sliced through the waves, allowed it to flow around him, he'd find it much easier.'

Marcus could see what he meant. 'Can we give that a go one day?'

Duggie nodded. 'Now's as good as any. Rescue boards just here. Grab one.'

Marcus nodded. He was a little nervous but keen to try. He hadn't told Tilly he could swim yet or that he'd done the last few evenings with Duggie. He'd avoided the mornings and her since their home-birth discussion. But each day he found he missed the rapport between them more as time passed. It seemed he'd enjoyed her company a lot.

Not to mention the fact that his body remembered the feel of her skin in the water. He missed that very much. Almost worth pretending he couldn't swim. She'd probably think they'd still need arm and leg movements in sections. He frowned at himself. Morally he couldn't do that.

He picked up the board. 'So who taught you about the ocean, Duggie?'

Duggie laughed. 'I learnt the hard way. The youngest of five brothers, they just threw me in.' His amusement split his face into a hundred weathered wrinkles and Marcus couldn't help smiling back. 'If I didn't learn, I went under. Was the youngest surf lifesaving champion in Australia thanks to those brothers.'

His craggy face saddened for a moment. 'Lost 'em all in the war. Didn't like being young then.' He picked up his board as if it were a feather. 'Come on. I'll show you how not to drown when you go to help someone.'

Marcus winced at the 'D' word and tucked his board under his arm. If someone had told him a month ago he'd be doing this he would have said they were mad. But one rise of Duggie's bushy white eyebrows and he was nodding his head. It was crazy how much confidence the old guy inspired.

The sea was warmer than the pool and the feel of the board under him as he paddled out after Duggie felt curiously liberating. His hands dug satisfyingly through the water and every few seconds he skimmed up a wave and down the other side. He could feel the stretch of his smile, the salt tingled on his face with the wind and he sucked in the sudden freedom of endless ocean in front of him. So this was why Tilly swam.

'Come alongside,' Duggie called back, and Marcus dug deeper.

Duggie slipped off the board and they practised the way to load victims and paddle back to the beach by riding a wave or kneeling. It was a little bit precarious and Marcus hoped he'd never need to use the knowledge, but it all gelled with Duggie's wisdom of being prepared.

CHAPTER NINE

AVOIDING Tilly at work was easier as time went on. That was a good thing. Dr Bennett and the midwife would never see eye to eye. He was busy, she was busy, and he could avoid her quite easily if he saw her in the distance. Something he'd mastered recently. He had no doubt she was avoiding him, too.

Mornings still lacked something, though. As if his brain refused to join the two Matildas and insisted on two different identities, and one of them he sorely missed. Mornings with Matilda were gone and it didn't feel right.

He'd achieved the reality by the simple expedient of running in another location but there was no doubt he felt the loss of the rapport they'd fallen into. He'd never felt that need with a woman before. To sit, talk, laugh.

The other was easier to understand because apparently the subtle sexual tension since that first kiss and during their one swimming lesson had been highlights of his year. He could tell because those memories intruded far too often into his thoughts when he ran. Even at the new beach.

Even now he could imagine the tangle of legs they'd ended with as he'd learnt to float, the softness of her breasts against the back of his head, and the feel of her hands against his skin. He wanted it back. He wanted Morning Matilda back but he had to come to terms with the fact that work dynamics played a part in how he handled the progress or lack of progress in their relationship.

Did it really matter that she had radical beliefs as long as he had control at work? Was he sabotaging a blossoming friendship, a different kind of relationship from anything he'd ever had, for the sake of work when it didn't have to cross over to there?

The next morning Tilly walked up the footpath towards Hill Street and she could see that Marcus's car was still there. So he hadn't gone to work yet. He'd been leaving really early this week. And she hadn't seen him out for his run. She'd swear he hadn't run at all the past few days since he'd abandoned her after the rally.

Well, she wasn't chasing him. He was the moth and she was the flame—Ellie's mantra echoed diligently in her head. Not that she wanted a relationship, but she'd enjoyed his company. Outside work anyway.

'Hi, there.' Tilly jumped, almost guiltily, as the object of her thoughts came up behind her.

Tilly didn't comment on the fact he'd been missing at this time for the last few days. 'Hello, there, to you.'

'Are you still keen for swimming lessons?' He stopped and walked beside her.

She shrugged. 'I thought you might not want to do them any more.'

He was looking at her strangely. 'I have some good memories. Maybe tomorrow if you're not busy?'

It seemed she wasn't *persona non grata* any more. That was nice. Confusing, but she wasn't going to get excited about it. 'If you'd like. The water's been lovely the last few days.'

She wanted to tell him she knew about his mother and his sister but it wasn't the sort of thing you could drop into a conversation. Maybe she'd just leave it to mention in another lifetime.

He glanced at his watch. 'See you then. I have to go in early today.' He jogged off again and she watched him cover the distance to his house with his long strides.

The guy was like a roller-coaster but she couldn't deny she felt that extra spring in her step that had been lacking the last few days. She told herself it was just because she didn't like being at outs with anyone.

The next morning Marcus kicked with his feet hanging onto the side of the pool.

He couldn't believe he was there despite his misgivings, ignoring his professional beliefs to be with her. He was like one of those stupid insects drawn to the blue light. He knew it was going to hurt but he couldn't resist. The only good thing was that now he had the confidence he could swim, everything felt easy. He assured himself that kicking practice would strengthen his freestyle.

Some folks might say he was a bit devious after his successful lessons with Duggie during the evenings but he enjoyed watching Tilly being teacher too much to resist.

And so far it had been as delightful as he'd imagined and it hadn't taken much, some skin, a little laughter, and he'd felt strangely at peace again. They were both kicking side by side as they hung onto the pool edge when the question popped into his mind. 'So, tell me about your family.'

'I have my mum.'

'Tell me about your mother.' Splash, splash, splash.

Her splashing slowed. 'Why?' It took him a minute to realise.

Two big kicks from Marcus. 'Because I sure as heck can't figure you out. Maybe if I can understand your mother then I'll understand you.'

Her kick increased and she didn't say anything for half a minute. Water flew into the air as if she was trying to kick the water to death. 'You'd hate my mother.'

Good grief. He let his feet sink and stood up to look at her. 'How can you say that?'

Tilly stopped too and they faced each other, wary, like kids who'd splashed each other too much. 'She's a home-birth midwife, very militant, but also very caring of the women in her care.'

Okay. Maybe he would. No. Of course he wouldn't because she'd be like Tilly and he couldn't hate her if he tried. He had tried—and failed. 'Where does she live?'

'Wollongong. South of Sydney.'

His breath eased out of the side of his mouth with a little hiss he hoped she didn't hear. He turned away and rubbed the back of his suddenly stiff neck. For a horrible moment he'd thought she was going to say up where his parents had lived. Even thinking about it made him shudder. Her mother would be too young to be the one anyway. He dropped his shoulders and sighed.

That shone a little light on why she was how she was. She went on. 'We lived with my grandmother and the only men I really knew were partners of the women my mother and grandmother cared for. She was a home-birth midwife, too.'

Of course she was. And her great-great-grandmother was probably a white witch who delivered at home, too. He couldn't help it —he still had issues with that. But it didn't make him want to get out of the pool and leave her. He had come a long way.

'What about your father?'

She shrugged. 'Never met him. Didn't want to know about me. There's some irresponsible men around.'

Yep. Like his own father, and he wasn't enjoying the conversation any more. He really should work on those issues.

It was Matilda's turn to be curious. 'What about your family?'

'I don't see my parents much. They're not the most responsible people. My sister drowned when I was young and I don't think I ever really forgave them or myself.'

He'd never verbalised that in his life. Why on earth would he bring it up now? His phone rang from the side of the pool and Marcus decided it was a great excuse to drop the subject. He stubbed his toe on the uneven rock of the pool in his haste to get to it. He wiped his hands on the towel, picked up his phone, and almost said thank you instead of hello.

Tilly watched him. Something had happened there. At least he'd mentioned his past but she could see he still had issues to resolve about his family. Silently she thanked Mrs Bennett for the heads up. A stark warning this man wasn't ready to be emotionally involved with anyone.

And she was a little worried she was forgetting she didn't want that either. Maybe it wasn't worth trying to keep their friendship.

He blew hot and cold so much she was getting a chill. She should be used to his fluctuations by now. She was getting way too obsessed with this guy. Tilly ran back over the strange conversation and the shift when she'd mentioned...what?

Tilly climbed out, well aware there'd be no more lesson today, or maybe any day if he was going to give off the vibes he was shedding at the moment.

'I have to go,' he said. She could tell he wanted to say more. Maybe even so she'd understand there could never be anything between them. Well, that was okay because she got that. But apparently he couldn't get the words out. Instead he waved as he turned away.

'And you have to go because of the phone call, too,' she said to his back.

His car was gone when she arrived in Hill Street and Mrs Bennett was sitting on her veranda.

Tilly chewed her lip and decided she couldn't stand not knowing. 'Mrs Bennett?'

'Yes, Tilly, dear.'

She leaned on the gate. 'Can I ask you something?'

'Of course.'

'I've just had a strange conversation with Marcus.'

Her neighbour laughed. 'Only one, dear?'

Tilly smiled. 'Actually, we've had a few, but today was right up there.' She looked at Mrs Bennett and wondered if she really wanted to know more things that would make her care about Marcus.

'Does Marcus ever see his family?'

Mrs Bennett smiled wryly. 'I think I've seen more of him this month than they have for the last twenty years.'

Tilly tried not to let her confusion over Marcus affect her at work the next few days. Keeping distance between them helped but it became impossible when Stella Trainer came in on Wednesday evening.

'I haven't felt my baby move.' Stella and her husband appeared at the desk at the start of Tilly's shift.

Tilly came round the desk and nodded with a sympathetic smile. 'Then let's go and have a little listen, shall we? That way you can feel reassured. Babies often slow down as they get closer to birth.'

She ushered Stella into the assessment room and pulled her notes. 'When was the last time you saw Dr Bennett?'

'Yesterday.' She smiled tremulously. 'We heard the heartbeat then.'

'Okay. That's good.' Tilly smiled again but she had this horrible sinking feeling drawn from the absolute fear that radiated from the mother in front of her. This was more than concern, this was terror at an instinctual level, and Tilly didn't like it.

She helped Stella lie down and lifted her floral maternity top to palpate her tummy to establish the lie of the baby. There was no movement with that stimulation so she applied a little more gel than she normally would and placed the Doppler over the spot where the baby's shoulder, and under that, baby's heart, would be situated and searched for the sound they both strained to hear.

Nothing. Tilly checked the other side and then back where she'd first listened. Still nothing.

'The heartbeat's not there. Is it?' Stella said flatly, with a horribly tight face and an anguished glance at her husband.

Tilly swallowed the fear in her own throat. 'I can't find it at the moment, Stella. I'm sorry. I'll get Gina, the midwifery manager, she's more experienced, and I'll page Dr Bennett to come down.'

Stella looked at her with bleak eyes. 'Thanks, Tilly. Yes, please.'

Tilly's mind raced as she almost ran out of the door. She found Gina talking to a relative and she tapped her shoulder. 'Excuse me. I'm sorry. I need you, please.'

Gina nodded to the relative and as she turned away Tilly whispered what had happened. Gina patted Tilly's shoulder. 'I'll go in while you ring Dr Bennett.'

When Marcus picked up the phone he almost hoped it was Tilly, even though he'd promised himself he was going to avoid her like the plague. But this was a Tilly he'd never heard.

'Dr Bennett. Stella Trainer has arrived with no foetal movement. I can't hear a foetal heart.' Her voice broke.

'I'm on my way.' No. Not Stella. He'd seen her yesterday. He should have done that bloody Caesarean last week.

The next two hours were tragic. The ultrasound proved that Stella's baby had died, though it couldn't say why or when. There was no signs of foetal distress, no apparent problems with the cord or placental separation. Just an unexplained cruel act of nature.

Stella and her husband perched on the edge of their chairs in stunned silence while Marcus sat helplessly, unable to give them a concrete reason or any hope that they were mistaken. All he could give them was sympathy and try to answer any questions the best he could.

He offered a Caesarean or an immediate induction

of the labour but gently recommended they wait a few days for Stella to go into labour naturally. Tilly silently nodded her agreement of this plan, too, and with trepidation the grieving parents decided to go home and wait for contractions to start.

Tilly gave them her mobile phone number if they needed to talk. Marcus had already done that.

Tilly glanced across at Marcus, his face a tight mask as they both watched the parents leave. He opened his mouth to say something, thought better of it and shook his head. Then he walked away. Tilly knew what he was thinking and her heart was breaking for everyone.

The next morning, after a night spent dozing in fits and starts in her bed, it was with relief that Tilly saw the streaks of dawn finally appear. She'd worried at the idea that her encouragement to Stella and Rob had cost their baby her life, though the fact that all had been well the previous day disputed that.

She knew it wasn't rational, she knew she was being unfair to herself, but common sense didn't help.

What if their baby had been born earlier? If she hadn't been on shift, would it still be alive? The horrible self-recriminations wouldn't go away. She dragged herself out of bed and pulled on her swimmers and then Tilly beat the water of the bay with tears streaming down her face. Instead of looking for dolphins, she almost wished a shark would gobble her up.

Despite her brief maudlin death wish, after her swim

she felt a little better and even a little calmer as she pushed through the breakers to the beach.

Until she saw the man doing slow laps in the sea pool. Marcus? Swimming? It wasn't graceful but it was strong. The slow strokes mechanical, repetitious, as if they could go on all day without effort. As if he was trying to exhaust himself and couldn't.

When had he learnt? Had he always known and he'd just lied to her? And the fact he was practising there in front of her was a message. She shook her head. She didn't understand but it was another blow to her morale. Tilly hurried past the pool and up to her house. She didn't want to see him because she'd just burst into tears.

Stella went into labour that night. She spoke to Tilly on her mobile and told her she wanted to stay home as long as she could because she didn't want medicated pain relief.

'If this is all I'm going to have when my baby is born, I want to feel the labour and remember it all.'

Tilly nodded into the phone and cleared her throat. 'Of course.' She could see that made sense. 'I'll have everything ready when you come in.' Tilly arranged for one of the other midwives to be available to take unobtrusive photographs if Stella wanted them.

Tilly was there waiting with the bath full and the lights dim when they arrived.

Stella's husband, Rob, had brought music they wanted to play. The lullabies they'd chosen with such anticipation for their baby's birth would still greet their little girl as she came into the world, even though she wouldn't hear them.

Tilly bit her lip and closed her eyes to get a grip. It was okay—maybe somewhere their baby would hear them.

Tilly checked Stella's observations and settled her into the bath, and even thought briefly about Marcus's preference for assessment of labour before Stella stepped in, but the mother preferred not to be disturbed and of course Tilly agreed.

'I need to ring Dr Bennett. Let him know you're in.'

'Okay. Thanks, Tilly.' Stella lay back with her eyes closed as she breathed through a contraction.

Tilly pulled the door shut gently, leaving them with the other midwife.

Tilly dialled Marcus's mobile and he answered at the second ring. 'Dr Bennett. It's Tilly.' She nearly said Sister McPherson but decided that was silly. 'Stella has arrived in established labour.' She thought she'd better tell him. 'She's in the bath.'

She heard the sigh. 'I don't suppose you examined her first?'

Tilly closed her eyes. 'She said she'd prefer not to be disturbed.'

'How convenient.' More irony than anger but still Tilly didn't need it.

'Don't do this, Marcus. We're all hurting. I'll ring you when she's pushing.' Tilly put the phone down gently.

Marcus snapped his phone shut. Well, he'd deserved that. But he was having real problems coping with Stella's loss. And it was even harder because he'd done everything right.

He'd monitored, scanned, checked the foetal growth and mother's health consistently. He'd done every conceivable blood test to ensure she was well. It wasn't fair. It wasn't right.

It didn't matter when people said some babies died. He knew what it was like to lose someone and he'd chosen this career to keep babies and mums safe. He'd failed. And he didn't know where or how not to do it again.

How could her baby have died? And the cancelled Caesarean only made it a hundred times worse. The ultimate case of 'if only'. He didn't think he'd ever forgive Matilda for talking Stella out of that, even though he knew it wasn't her fault. He began to dress to go up to the hospital.

His phone rang again and it was Tilly. 'She's pushing.'

'I'm coming,' he said, but the phone was dead. Tilly had already gone. Of course she wouldn't leave them long at this time.

When Marcus arrived he expected to find them out of the bathroom and pushing on the bed—but of course they weren't.

They were in the bathroom, the mother submerged in the water and Tilly on her knees, peering into the gloom. Stella was gently breathing her baby out.

He shut his mouth. What was he going to say? Get out or the baby will drown? Marcus drew a slow breath in and sighed. He nodded at Rob, who was in the bath, too, but seated behind his wife and holding her gently as Stella leaned back against him.

Marcus quietly moved to the only vacant seat in the room—the toilet. He vaguely noticed the other midwife in the corner with a camera.

He may as well watch and learn. In fact, when he thought about it, despite the muted sadness, it was very peaceful in here, pleasantly warm, and the light was dim but enough to see by. He noticed Tilly had a torch by her feet in case she needed to see, but otherwise not much was happening, and apparently that was fine.

'Keep breathing like that, Stella,' Tilly whispered. 'Now put your hands down and feel baby's head as she comes out.'

Good grief, they were at that stage? He couldn't tell by Stella's face.

'I can feel her,' Stella whispered.

'That's lovely. Keep breathing with the contractions until she glides into your hands.' Tilly gestured to Rob to stretch his hands around and feel if he could.

Tilly peered into the water. 'Here she comes.' She still hadn't put her hands in at all. It was all the parents. Marcus was spellbound. A little horrified but spellbound.

Then his brain suddenly remembered that this was in water. He hated water. Water had taken his little sister and it had been his fault. He should have looked after her.

But he'd been so small. Too young to have that responsibility. The voice came from nowhere. Never his fault. The voice was repeating it like a litany in his head and while his eyes watched the parents lift and greet their eternally sleeping baby, in some unexplained and mystical way he said goodbye to his own baby sister, and finally left her to rest in peace. Of course his parents had never blamed him. It had been beyond his control. As this was beyond his control.

This wasn't his fault. What Tilly said was true. He'd done everything he knew to keep mother and baby safe. It hadn't been enough, but it wasn't his fault. Or Tilly's. It wasn't anybody's fault. It was a tragic turn of nature.

He looked across to where Stella was holding her baby between her breasts in the water, tears in rivers down her cheeks and Rob's arms around them all.

Tilly had sat back, tears on her own face, and he didn't know when he moved, just that he did. He knelt behind her and put his arms around her waist until, after initial stiffness, she leant back against him.

They all stayed, in a tableau, as Stella held baby Katia until it was time to move.

Marcus left them a little while later. He'd checked Katia for any obvious reasons why she'd passed away inside her mother but none were obvious. There was nothing more he could do.

He left a remarkably composed Tilly to deal with

the touches he knew little about, wrote an initial brief comment in Stella's notes, and went back to his office.

He couldn't erase in his mind the view he'd had from where he'd sat. The tableau of composed grief set amidst the subdued wonder of an amazing birth. In this situation he could even be an advocate for delivery in water—yet he couldn't call it anyone delivering anything. It had been a mother aware of her body's force and capturing the moment to welcome her child into the world.

Such a tragedy the child hadn't been able to breathe the air when her face had lifted to the surface. He scrubbed his face as if to lose the frozen expression he knew was on there and sat down to write a detailed consultant's report which he would drop down later when he went to see Stella again.

Two hours later, Marcus went to see the parents. Stella and Rob were settled in a private room with Katia, whom they were keeping with them tonight while Stella stayed in hospital. He arranged to see them in his rooms when the results came back from the examination of Katia in a week's time and again offered his number if they needed to talk.

When he left them he couldn't see Tilly anywhere and the ward seemed remarkably quiet for a place that delivered half a dozen babies a day. He passed two other midwives but not Tilly, and he tried not to look for her but in the back of his mind he'd realised that such gentle strength for the parents would come at a cost. He worried about her—he couldn't help it.

He heard a sniff as he went past the cleaner's room, a tiny alcove with a door, and when he stopped outside he heard it again.

She was crying. He'd known it.

He lifted his hand but hesitated. What help would he be? If she hadn't wanted privacy she wouldn't have hidden away. But she was hurting. She wasn't the only one.

He knocked gently and pushed open the door. It was dark. Why on earth hadn't she put on the light?

'Matilda?'

She sniffed and he narrowed his eyes in the dimness, reached out and touched her face. The dampness ran down his fingers and he gently wiped big stripes of tears from her cheeks. She turned her head. 'It's my nose that needs wiping,' she muttered.

'Sorry, but I'm not using my fingers for that.'

He bit back a smile, just glad she had a bit of fight in her and wasn't totally destroyed. 'Take the handkerchief, please.' He pushed it into her hand.

'Thank you.' Muffled but sincere.

'You okay?'

She glared at him through the dimness. 'Why are you in my cupboard?'

He held back another urge to smile. 'It's my cupboard, too.'

She shook her head. 'Typical.'

He ignored her comment and went on. 'I'm here because my friend is in this cupboard. I thought you might need company.'

Even she smiled, albeit a little miserably, but he was glad to see it.

'It's a very small cupboard.'

He said, 'I just wanted to say you were amazing with Stella and Rob.' She sniffed again and unscrunched his handkerchief to use again.

She blew her nose loudly and he couldn't help the glance he cast over his shoulder at the door.

He realised just how damning this could look if they were caught in here, though what people could say if they found them was a long way from Tilly's mind. 'If she'd had the Caesarean, the baby might still be alive.'

He didn't want to think about that. He couldn't be-cause—he just couldn't. 'We don't know that. If we're very lucky the post-mortem will tell us, but you know how often the reason for stillbirth is never found.'

There was a silence he had to fill. 'The birth was very special.'

She lifted her head. 'Even though it was a water birth?'

'In this case I can see the absolute benefits.' He needed to get out of here, in any direction, but he couldn't seem to move.

He reached out and brushed the damp hair off her face. This was ridiculous. Two tall people cramped in a cupboard with cleaning materials, mops, vases, and dead flowers.

He leant forward and brushed her forehead in a kiss. 'I just wanted you to know I thought the birth was beautiful.' He was repeating himself.

So he left.

Tilly knew Marcus blamed her. How could he not? But that was okay because she hadn't stopped beating herself up. She didn't think she could face him, or anyone else, at the minute. Thank goodness it was almost eleven and she could go home.

She was meeting Ruby to share a taxi and hopefully she could get home without bursting into tears. This job could give the most joy and, at moments like this, the most pain. But she wouldn't change being there for Stella and Rob. Not in a million years, but she couldn't help but wonder if Marcus felt the same.

'Poor Tilly.' They were in the kitchen at Hill Street and Ruby put her arms around Tilly and gave her a big hug. Sympathetic tears glinted in her eyes, too. 'Poor you. You do an awesome job. I'd want you there if I was them, and of course it's not your fault.'

'I know, but I feel so guilty. I don't even want to go into work tomorrow.'

Ruby nodded. 'I know. I felt the same last month when that six-year-old came into Emergency after that house fire. It breaks your heart watching other people's pain. You listen and try to support them and somewhere inside it rips your heart a little and even though we're not directly involved it does take a little time to heal. God knows how the ambulance officers do it time after time. No wonder they burn out.' They both shuddered.

Ruby sat the chocolate biscuits in front of Tilly. 'Here. Have the lot.'

'Not the emergency chocolate ration?' Tilly laughed through her tears. 'I get to have the whole box?'

'I'm thinking about it.' Ruby pretended to hover her hand indecisively over the box. 'Better hurry before I change my mind.'

Tilly pushed the chocolate away. 'Actually, I feel sick.' She stood up and hugged Ruby. 'Thanks for being here. And I'm so sorry I didn't know about last month. You didn't tell me about your six-year-old.'

Ruby hugged her back and she put the biscuits back up on top of the cupboard. If they weren't going to help then they didn't need the calories. 'Cort was there. We did our grieving together.'

'You're so lucky.' Tilly chewed her lip. 'I'm thinking I might ask Gina for a week off to go and see my mum.'

Ruby nodded. 'Things not working out with Marcus?'

Tilly shook her head. 'I don't want to talk about that either.'

Ruby patted her arm. 'I think going to your mum's is a great idea.'

After four days, Marcus decided he needed help to find Tilly. She wasn't at work, not around the house, repairing or painting something, and the girls next door avoided him so he couldn't catch them to ask, and his aunt didn't know.

He'd watched vigilantly for her each morning but he hadn't seen her slip out for her swim or stroke her way across the bay.

He'd kept up the swimming lessons with Duggie

and the old man had begun to teach him butterfly and backstroke and he'd had his first surf. He'd have liked to tell Tilly about it.

That morning he'd cracked and asked Gina where she was when he'd done his morning round.

'She's gone to her mother's for a week. Stella's loss upset her.' Gina looked at him. 'Her mother's a friend of mine. She's a home-birth midwife, you know.'

Marcus felt the usual kick from that statement but it wasn't as bad. Not right through his gut anyway. 'I know.' Such a twist of fate but not as important today. Maybe it wasn't the final nail in the coffin of a relationship with Tilly he'd thought it was, because at the moment he was more interested in catching up with her again and seeing that she was all right. He needed to make sure she wasn't blaming herself.

Three days later Marcus was in his office. 'Mr and Mrs Trainer are here to see you, Doctor.' Marcus stood up and greeted Stella and Rob. She carried a small silver folder and to his surprise she kissed his cheek.

She looked subdued but remarkably composed. 'How are you, Stella? Rob?'

Rob answered for her. 'We're both well, Doctor. And you?'

'Fine.' He gestured to the two chairs facing his desk and pulled the one out from behind so he could sit next to them.

Rob gestured to his wife. 'Stella was worried about you.'

'Thank you, Stella.' How could she have a skerrick of emotion left for him? 'I felt your loss very much.' He looked at the pathologist's summary in his hands with mixed feelings and decided to get on with it.

'I have the report back from Katia's examination.' He waited while they absorbed that and seemed ready for him to go on.

Rob reached over and took Stella's hand then indicated they were ready. Marcus didn't doubt he wasn't the only one who found it hard to speak at the moment.

He cleared his throat. 'Katia had a brain haemorrhage, an uncommon and untreatable aneurism, or extreme weakness in the wall of the blood vessel that surrounded her brain.' The parents looked at each other and Stella wiped a lone tear away impatiently.

Marcus went on. 'The examining doctor...' they all tried not to think about that '...seemed to think that even a Caesarean birth would not have prevented the rupture and he was surprised she'd grown so well and for so long inside your uterus.'

Rob swallowed. 'So not compatible with life?'

Marcus nodded. 'The blood-vessel wall seemed to have whole areas of extreme congenital weakness so I'm afraid not.'

Stella sat forward. 'So, in fact, if she'd been born by Caesarean we may not have had that time with her, the tranquillity of her arrival, the calmness to savour that precious time with her.'

Marcus thought about that. There was no doubt that could be true. 'I hadn't thought about that but you're probably right. Of course, there would have been extreme measures used to try and save Katia if the aneurysm had ruptured at birth because we wouldn't have known what was wrong with her.' He nodded. 'Yes, it could have been very traumatic.'

Stella sat back and glanced at her husband. 'That's very comforting.'

Marcus nodded again. It was. A gentle waft of peace crept over him as if a cloud had drifted away and allowed warmth from the sun to suddenly stream in the window. 'I think so, too.' He looked at Stella. 'Do you have any questions?'

Stella smiled sadly. 'We'll always have questions but that's not why we're here.' She glanced at her husband. 'Perhaps we could ring you if we have more?' Rob nodded.

'Of course.' Marcus included them both in his agreement. 'Any time. If I'm not here, I'll phone you back as soon as I can.'

Stella took a deep breath and let it out slowly. 'Thank you for that.'

She tightened her hands around the little book on her lap. 'I wanted to show you the beautiful memories we have of Katia.

'There were parts of that two days we spent in hospital that were a blur and parts that will remain treasured memories. Thanks to Tilly and the other midwives and to you for being so generous with all the time you spent with us.'

Marcus swallowed the lump in his throat. 'To borrow

Matilda's words, it was a privilege to be there with you both for Katia's birth.'

Stella glanced down at the folder. 'Thank you. I hope you don't mind but I've brought our daughter's things to show you.'

She opened the first page and lifted several black-and-white photographs in baby frames, photos of Stella in the birth pool with Katia snuggled against her mother moments after her birth. Rob's arms encircled them all and the picture could have been of any birth.

The tenderness on both parents' faces pulled hard on Marcus's composure.

'And this is Katia's hand-and footprints. Tilly did a good job, don't you think?' The little outlines were clean and stark against the thick white paper and incredibly touching.

Next she handed him a frame with a little white plaster cast of a clenched baby fist and a tiny foot, and then Stella lifted a smaller album with pink rabbits gambolling on the front. He didn't know how much more of this he could take. She passed it to him.

Photographs of Katia, photos of each parent holding their daughter. His throat caught and when he turned the page and saw one of Tilly, tears glistening at the corners of her beautiful eyes and the precious bundle of Katia wrapped in a hand-sewn rug in her arms, he could feel the thickness in his throat.

Someone had even taken one of him, an intense expression on his face as he looked towards the bath, and it brought back the poignancy and the tragedy of that day. And another of his back as he hugged Tilly and the parents in front of them both with their baby.

He couldn't imagine how many times this little baby's mother must have already looked at these and how many more there were to come over the next years. Over the rest of her life, probably.

He carefully handed back the album. 'Katia's photos are incredibly beautiful. Thank you for showing me.'

'Thank you for being there.'

All Marcus could think about was that he wanted to see Tilly. He wanted to tell her about the pathology results. Tell her about Stella's folder. Tell her and see the same comfort in her eyes as there was in Stella and Rob's and his own, after understanding the report.

*

CHAPTER TEN

TILLY came back to work on Friday and she didn't see Marcus because he'd gone to a meeting in the city. That was a good thing because she wasn't sure she wouldn't cry when she did.

Her mum had been wonderful, had had sage advice for dealing with grieving parents and cautioned Tilly about losing her heart to a man who blamed her for something that wasn't her fault. She wasn't a hundred per cent sure her mother understood how she felt about Marcus but, then again, neither did she. But the solution to the problem was the same. Stay away from him.

It was midnight and Tilly and Ruby had just arrived home from work. Tilly was making cocoa and they were both on the early shift the next morning.

Ruby put her hand on Tilly's shoulder. 'You look worried, Till.'

Tilly smiled ruefully. 'I'm a real life of the party. Sorry to mope around. I haven't seen Marcus yet. Not since Stella lost her baby.'

'You said he was good in the cupboard.'

Tilly had to smile at how strange that sounded. 'Yes, he was good in the cupboard. But I've decided I don't want to see Marcus out of work. Now Mary's asked me to speak to Marcus about being the back-up consultant for a home-birth client and I don't know what to do.'

Ruby brought down the secret hoard of chocolate biscuits again and put two in front of Tilly. 'Why did she ask you?'

Absently Tilly nibbled the edge of one. 'Because I work with him, I guess. Mary's agreed to take the mum on if she'll see a consultant as well.'

Ruby sat down. 'So what's the problem? Ask him.'

Tilly ticked the evils off on her fingers. 'Number one, I haven't spoken to him since I left. Number two, apparently his mother nearly died in a bungled home birth, which I'm not supposed to know, and he hates anything to do with them. And, three, I don't want to get shut down. It hurts.'

Ruby put her arm around Tilly and hugged her. 'Poor you.' She scrutinised her. 'You're having a tough couple of weeks. Plus you still really like him, don't you?'

'Too much. Which is dumb because I don't trust him not to hurt me. And I promised myself I wasn't going to fall into the same old trap with another guy. Especially one older then me. Friends only.'

'Easier said than done. Men are risky. And I can understand your reluctance. Though he's not technically old. He's the same age as Cort.' Her face softened and she smiled a small secret smile. 'But sometimes the risk is worth it.'

Tilly had to laugh. 'You're just saying that because it's worked out for you and Cort.'

Ruby grinned. 'Probably true. I'm happy. The happiest I've ever been and I know it's going to get even better. But it's not about me.' Ruby put down her cup. 'Can you trust him a little bit, Till?'

She sighed. 'Every time I do he comes up with another reason why it won't work. So I've decided to stay out of his way. Plus he's out of my league.'

'Excuse me.' Ruby looked down her nose at Tilly's preposterous statement. 'I'm not out of Cort's league any more than Marcus is out of yours. He'd be darned lucky to have someone as gorgeous and genuine as you are in his life.'

Tilly brushed that away. 'It's all right for you—your brother's work with plastic surgery is famous and your father was a top surgeon, too. My mum's a second-generation home-birth midwife.'

She shrugged that problem away. 'Anyway, the trouble is if I don't ask him for Mary and something goes wrong, it'll be a hundred times worse, and not just for the client. Plus it leaves Mary in the lurch.'

Ruby nodded. 'I say ask him. Make it short and he can ask questions if he decides to think about it. He might be different since Stella's baby.'

Tilly sighed heavily. 'I can't imagine why.'

The next day Tilly watched him from the corner of the ward. Unobtrusively. Nervously. Marcus talking to Gina. He'd finished the ward round, his registrar and resident had departed for the antenatal clinics, and Tilly knew he'd leave for his rooms soon. She wanted to pass on Mary's request, get it off her chest, and she wanted to do it at work.

Marcus left the nurses' station with his eyes on his phone, checking his diary. He'd been thinking about Tilly and he'd had a dozen light-bulb moments about the way she made him feel.

A tiny smile twitched—like lighter and calmer and more philosophical instead of totally relying on control to run his life, which was lucky because when he was with Tilly things seemed to get out of control pretty darned fast.

He'd never be a thrill seeker or a big risk taker and he never wanted to change that his work would always be methodical and thorough.

But he was coming to realise that Tilly, and by association the other midwives, had his patients' best interests at heart and he could be more open to new ideas.

Perhaps even learn to surrender a little of the control he'd felt he needed to apply over his private life, too. He'd always gone for women who were happy for a man to arrange everything and that had suited his tendency to make all the decisions.

He didn't feel like that at the moment. He felt like he wanted to step onto the whirligig with Tilly. Sit in a room and sing impromptu songs. Seize the moment and kiss her until they were both senseless. Maybe jump in his car and just drive for the pleasure of having her next to him, no matter where they ended up.

A month ago that wouldn't have seemed even possible let alone the ridiculous attraction that idea held for him now. He'd have to arrange a meeting with her. Try and find out how she felt before he made a fool of himself.

'Dr Bennett?' He had his finger on the elevator button and it hovered without pressure as she spoke.

Marcus turned. Ah, there she was. He hadn't expected her on this shift. Finally. And gorgeous. It was good to see her, though she looked a little careworn for such a young woman. Like she needed a hug. Lucky he was at work then.

'Hello, there, Matilda. Long time no see. I've been trying to catch up with you.'

Before she could distract him he went on. 'Actually, I've wanted to sit down and talk to you but the time's flown since I found out. I think you need to know as soon as possible.'

He saw her frown, as if she wondered what else she'd done wrong now. It was surprising how unhappy that made him feel. 'Don't look like that. Am I such an ogre?' She didn't answer and he sighed and thought maybe he was. Nothing he could do about it at this minute. He needed to say this. 'Stella and Rob came to see me.'

Tilly brushed a strand of escaping hair off her face. 'I haven't had a chance to ring her since I got back. How are they?'

Typical, Marcus thought, worried about others when the cost on her was so evident. Hopefully this would help.

'The pathology came back and Katia had a congenital aneurism incompatible with life. It's unlikely she would have survived a Caesarean and the resuscitation would have been much more traumatic than the beautiful birth she had.'

He felt again a little of the relief he'd felt the first time he'd read that and he saw Tilly soak in the concept. Tears glistened in her eyes and he wished now he'd taken her up to his rooms, but he wasn't sure he would have been able to stop himself hugging her if he had. Not good to do that at work, even in the privacy of his office. Self-protection.

'So it wasn't because Stella decided to have the normal birth. It wasn't my fault Katia died.'

'It never was, Matilda,' Marcus said quietly. 'I wasn't as supportive as I should have been but it was never your fault. It was all beyond our control. Yours, mine, Stella's.'

She drew a deep breath and he had that urge to hug her again. Instead, he just tightened his hold on his mobile.

She nodded and looked away. 'Thank you for telling me.'

'I wish I could have done it somewhere else.' He shouldn't have been such a coward.

She lifted her head. 'No. This is good. And I'll think about it more later.'

It wasn't quite the response he'd thought he'd get. He'd hoped she'd look more relieved or something. 'If you have any questions, you'll ask, won't you?'

She nodded and brushed her eyes. Then she straightened her shoulders. 'I do have something to ask you. Not related to Stella.'

Marcus was still beating himself up over the way he'd handled that. Protecting himself rather than Tilly, a poor effort, and he promised himself he'd never do that again.

Tilly wasn't sure she had his full attention. But she wanted this out of the way so she went on doggedly. 'Do you remember the home-birth midwife, Mary, from your second day?'

'Yes. I have a memory of lots of things.' He smiled at her and she almost lost her train of thought. What was that supposed to mean? He added, 'She seemed a sensible woman.'

Tilly looked at him in surprise. Had they progressed to that? What was going on here? Maybe he had changed.

'Anyway, Mary has a client who's reluctant to see any doctor, isn't risk free, and Mary wanted me to ask if you would see her with the view of shared care.' Out it came in a rush, a little garbled, and as she finished speaking she tried to sense his possible reaction but couldn't.

His brows creased but not badly. She was a basket case, reading nuances when there wasn't any and second-guessing his reactions. What had happened to the woman who'd declared they weren't handmaidens? The one who'd give anyone an earful if they looked sideways at one of her birthing women. Maybe she'd learnt to see both sides a little more. Imagine that.

Marcus nodded but it was pushing reality to think he said it encouragingly. 'So this mother's high risk and wants to birth at home and you think I should agree to that.'

She'd known this would be hard. 'No. Mary wants to discuss the case with you because she's worried if she doesn't care for her, this mum will go for a home birth with just her husband.'

'I see.' Well, she certainly had his attention. Tilly tried not to squirm. 'Then why isn't she asking me?'

Good point. But she'd come this far. 'I'll tell her to ring your secretary then.'

Marcus studied her noncommittally and Tilly waited. 'Very adroitly handled, Sister.'

A tiny smile that warmed her more than it should. 'Fine. Get her to ring my secretary and we can talk about it.' He pushed the button and the doors opened. Just before they closed he said, 'There's something I want to talk to you about. And we need to discuss carpetbag steak at some point, too.'

When the doors had closed Tilly sagged back against the wall. Marcus at work was so much harder to handle. Except she wasn't going to handle him outside the hospital any more. Ever again.

'What was all that about?' Gina looked up as Tilly approached the desk.

Tilly blinked, still relieved he hadn't shut her down and a little bemused about the steak comment. She wasn't going to take him up on that one. She needed some space and that was definitely an outside-work commitment. 'Mary asked me if he'd see a client of hers as shared care.'

Gina's brows rose. 'Good grief. We have progressed. Well done.'

It was almost the end of the shift when a call came in from another home-birth midwife. Again Tilly was the one to ring Marcus, although the afternoon staff would take over from her in that actual OT. 'Dr Bennett?'

'Yes, Matilda.'

Well, he certainly knew her voice. 'We have a mother coming in from home with foetal distress and the midwife is requesting we prepare for an emergency Caesarean on their arrival.' Tilly wasn't the only one who was aware of the irony on top of the emergency situation.

'Put Theatres on standby.' She had the feeling he was smiling into the phone. 'I'll assess the woman but you get Theatre started. Of course I trust you.'

Yee-ha. 'Thank you.' But it was too late for her. She didn't trust him.

Almost a week after Tilly had come back from her mother's they still hadn't seemed to connect for their morning exercise, which was particularly frustrating when he'd decided he wanted to tell Matilda about his sister. Marcus had decided it was time to try to explain his reservations.

He'd stayed with his exercise time in the mornings but he had the feeling that Tilly had adjusted hers to avoid him. He guessed that was tit for tat. And she was avoiding him very successfully.

She had more leeway with working mostly in the afternoons and even at work his schedule was conspiring against him. He'd had a run of evening meetings and no unexpected birth call-backs at night so he'd seen little of her except in the distance, apart from that conversation at the lift.

He couldn't go chasing her all over the ward, especially when he had the feeling she was ducking into rooms to avoid him.

That morning, before his run, he'd decided to find out if she was waiting for him to leave for work before she went. A meeting at eleven o'clock in the city meant no early round this morning. His registrar rang him to say he had it all covered, just as he heard Matilda's gate open, and Marcus had to watch her walk away from his bedroom window.

'Ring me if needed, otherwise I'll be in late this afternoon.' He ended the call and took the stairs two at a time to try to catch her before she hit the water.

It was after eight when Tilly opened the gate to slip down for her swim. Marcus's car was still there but she'd waited long enough. He'd have no time before work now and she wasn't as happy with the later hour when the beach had more people and her peace often became interrupted by other swimmers appearing beside her through a wave when she least expected it.

But it was worth it to avoid the chance of running into him.

She'd decided she was going cold turkey.

No contact. She'd started painting the kitchen in the house and apart from her brief forays into the water after he'd gone to work, she'd mostly avoided him by being aware of where he was at all times when she was on the ward.

She chose to care for patients who were under different doctors, opted for women in earlier labour, and, when she'd asked, Gina helped to keep the two apart.

The whitecaps were blowing off the back of the waves this morning and she could see a small rip across her usual traverse.

Tilly glanced towards the walled ocean pool but she was fed up with being dictated to by events she couldn't control. Stubbornly she headed a little east of her usual trajectory and splashed through the breakers.

It wasn't long before she realised she hadn't swum wide enough and the undertow was stronger than she liked. She drifted a bit farther out to sea to avoid the centre of a wider-than-average rip but soon realised she was caught anyway.

'Bother,' she muttered as she drifted even farther out, the cold logic of experience telling her not to try to swim out of the rip but to let it carry her until the current stream naturally stopped. It was the first thing she taught the Nippers and junior lifesavers.

Of course, the rip could peter out and drop her in the next bay and she'd have to walk back, but there wasn't a lot she could do about it unless she wanted to exhaust herself uselessly trying to fight the strength of the current.

That was when the shark siren went off. Tilly heard the high-pitched wail of the beach siren and it took a moment until she realised what it was.

The accepting calm she'd just been congratulating herself on suddenly faltered and her already accelerated heart rate jumped another twenty beats. Her head swivelled as she peered into the water closest to her with a dread she tried to control.

She couldn't believe that the first rip she'd been caught in this year had to come at the same time as the siren. There was no way she could get to the beach fast, and if she panicked and thrashed her way through it she'd be a more noisy target for whichever shark had decided that Coogee was a great place to visit.

Funny how the skin on her legs seemed suddenly more sensitive. How the sound of her own breathing was rasping more loudly through her throat until it seemed almost raucous in the morning air. With great difficulty she consciously slowed the kicking of her legs to what she hoped was an unobtrusive up and down glide as she floated as passively as she could with the current.

It would be nice to be able to put her hand up and wait for one of the beach-patrol lifesavers to gun the rubber ducky boat and save her, but it was still too early for them to be out and about and she didn't want some novice being a hero and drowning for her.

Maybe with the shark alarm there was hope the real guys would start earlier.

She glanced around fearfully again. Where was a dolphin when she needed one? The siren sounded again and she closed her eyes and only just resisted the urge to kick into the current towards the shore. Her brain knew the rip was much stronger than she was and the only answer was to allow it to carry her where it wanted before it petered out.

She could feel the waves of nervous energy bleating against her common sense and her legs itched to kick like crazy for the shore.

A wave slapped her in the face and a little more of her composure fled. For the first time since she'd begun swimming in the mornings she raised her arm and hoped for rescue.

CHAPTER ELEVEN

MARCUS looked around when the alarm went off but he had no idea what it meant.

Until a young tattooed man in a wheelchair spun to the edge of the path with a loud hailer pointed out to sea. 'Please get out of the water. Return to the shore. This is a shark alarm.'

Marcus felt as if one of those surfboards heading for the beach had sneaked up on him and punched him in the chest. Tilly was out there. He glanced around to see others hurrying for the shore but Tilly seemed to be drifting farther out as he watched. Why wasn't she coming in?

He jogged over to the man with the microphone and pointed out Tilly. 'Can she hear you?'

'She'd hear the siren anyway.' He frowned out to where Tilly drifted. 'Must be caught in a rip.' He shook his head as Marcus's gut clenched at the words. 'At least she's sensible not to fight it and the sharks are on the other side of the bay.'

He pointed and Marcus could see two dark fins

gliding through the water. There was something men-
acing in the way they sliced the water like a knife as
they lazily circled to the left side of the bay.

The man went on. 'I'm a volunteer spotter until the
lifesavers come in. Not much I can do. I've rung them
and they should be here in about ten minutes.'

A shark could eat Tilly in ten minutes if it decided to
investigate her. He glanced at the big emergency Malibu
leaning against the pole. 'Can I take the rescue board?'

The man shrugged. 'If you're keen on finding the
shark. The boys'll have the rubber ducky up and going
in twenty.'

Duggie had told him of the days before rubber duck-
ies. Of bronzed men swimming with floats and paddling like machines out on their boards to rescue people
in rips. He could have lived without the experience but
he was quietly confident that if he stayed with the board
he could be a help, not a hindrance, to Tilly. The shark
he didn't want to think about.

He lifted the board and hugged it against his body
as he balanced it under his armpit like he had with
Duggie. People hurried from the water and glanced at
him strangely as he walked past them to push into the
waves.

'Didn't you hear the alarm, mate?' A thin, elderly
gentleman indicated the man in the wheelchair.

'Yes, thanks.' He didn't want to talk. He wanted to
concentrate on the quickest way to Tilly and as he gauged
the direction and distance he saw her put her hand up for
help just before a wave obscured her from view.

He narrowed his eyes and any doubts he had fled. She was tiring. He couldn't imagine what was going though her mind after hearing the alarm. Or maybe he could because there were some pretty graphic pictures circling in his head.

Tilly was starting to panic. She'd bitten her lip and it was the taste of blood in her mouth that really scared her. Imagine if she'd let some drop into the water. Duggie had once told her a shark could smell blood a quarter of a mile away and she wished like anything she hadn't been able to remember that little fact.

The swell seemed bigger the farther out she drifted because she lost sight of the beach between the waves. Her sense of isolation grew and thoughts of drifting right out to sea were beginning to crowd her mind. Nobody knew she was there. She was alone. With sharks.

She could die. Finished. Eaten by a shark. The first things she'd know would be a jolting drag as it chewed off her leg. Her friends would be devastated. What about Marcus? Would he care? Why the heck had she been fooling herself she hadn't fallen in love with the man? She should have taken what she could while she could. He'd been looking for her for days and now she had plenty of time to regret lost opportunity. A broken heart was nothing to being eaten by a shark.

Tears mixed with seawater. She'd give her last breath to be in his arms. No matter that he didn't love her. She knew he liked her. At least she would've died happy. She was such a fool.

By the time Marcus reached her she would have clutched the Grim Reaper himself. Avoiding Marcus was the last thing she wanted to do. She kicked towards him and finally she could touch the board. His hand came down over hers and squeezed her fingers and the warmth and strength and calmness began to seep into her panicked mind.

'Marcus? Thank God.' Then she shook her head. 'I can't believe it's you. Am I dreaming?'

'If you are, can we do it when we get to shore?'

She squeezed his hand harder to reassure herself he really was there and his bones were solid beneath her fingers. 'You can use the board?'

'Yeah, I can. Great teacher.' He pulled parallel to the beach. 'Put your arm over the board and grab the hand rope and I'll pull your legs in front of me.'

'I can't believe you came out to get me.'

'Why wouldn't I?' He smiled at her wryly. 'You'd come for me, wouldn't you?'

'Not with a shark alarm maybe.' A brave attempt at a joke.

He bit back a laugh. At least she was honest. He slid carefully down the end of the board, trying not to think of his feet dangling in the water, and ended up lying between her legs. It was amazingly easy to paddle with his hands and Tilly was paddling, too.

They both had good reason to get into the beach as fast as they could.

Obviously the board was designed for this because it didn't seem to have any problems carrying the two of them.

'It wasn't as tricky getting you on here as I thought it might be.' He could hear the relief in his voice as he turned the board back towards the beach, away from the side with the sharks.

'It's easier if your victim knows what they're doing. I've done it before and got the idea.' He could hear a quiver in her voice and he didn't blame her. He'd bet he'd have felt like that, too, if he'd been alone at sea and imagining getting washed up in New Zealand, like she must have.

All he wanted to do was gather her up and hug her. But he couldn't. They needed to get to the shore before some curious shark decided to have breakfast. But he would hug her. My word, he would.

A small swell lifted them and helped glide them back towards the shore, and he paddled the board straighter to catch the next one as well. Suddenly they were gliding swiftly through the water towards the crowd on the beach.

The rubber ducky had been pulled out onto the sand and he could see the lifesavers with caps waiting at the beach. They stopped to watch him come in with Tilly on the board and two of them waded out to help as they reached the shallows.

'You okay, Tilly?' The stocky lifesaver took her hand as she slid off and helped her stand. She nodded and he helped her out of the water up to the sand.

The second lifesaver took hold of the hand rope. 'Well done, sir. I'll take the board if you want.'

'Thanks.' Marcus nodded and took two big strides until he'd caught up with Tilly. When he put his hand on her shoulder she turned and looked at him. The lifesaver must have seen something in his face because he dropped Tilly's hand like a hot potato and went back to help his friend.

'Come here.' His voice softened at the paleness in her face. He hadn't realised how pale she was out there, and he just wanted to crush her against him.

She stepped into his arms and he hugged her into his chest. 'You came for me,' she mumbled against his chest, and the vibration made him smile.

'Of course.' She felt cold and shaky and he hugged her tighter. 'You okay, honey?'

She nodded and her hair brushed his chin. 'The rip I could deal with but not a shark.'

'I'd have had hysterics if it was me.' He dropped a kiss on top of her head.

She stepped back and tilted her head to look at him. 'It was you. You risked your own safety and saved me. You didn't have to.'

'Don't talk about it.' Actually, he didn't want to even think about it. 'You might have turned me off water again.'

'Who showed you how to use the board?'

'Duggie's been coaching me while you were playing hide and seek.'

She shot him a look of surprise. 'Sneak.' Then she shuddered. 'I'm very glad.'

He turned her towards home with his arm around her shoulders. 'Come on. You need a hot shower and some food. The girls will look after you.'

She couldn't stop shaking. 'Everyone's working.'

'Good. I'll look after you.' He sounded quite pleased, Tilly thought vaguely as she moved through a wall of vibrating cotton wool that seemed to be wrapping around her legs thicker and thicker so that she moved more clumsily the farther they went.

Each step up the hill she took the more the delayed shock drained her energy until she seemed to barely move. She couldn't get the thought of the shark out of her mind but funnily enough it was the idea of Marcus putting himself in danger that scared her most.

Pictures of Marcus and thrashing water circled like predators in her head and she shuddered.

He must have felt the vibration because he pulled her closer into his side. 'You okay?' He peered into her face and she'd bet she was whiter than a sheet. She stumbled.

'Can you make it? Do you want me to carry you?'

Yes, please, she thought. 'We're almost there.' She glanced ahead and the gate seemed a mile away.

He scooped her up in his arms like he had the day the hammer had hit her toe and it felt just as good the second time. Better. She closed her eyes and sighed into him. He was damp where he'd pulled his shirt on over his wet body but warm already and irresistibly safe and solid, and she pushed her ear against his chest and listened to the sound of his heart against her ear lobe.

It was incredibly reassuring. Now the gate was too close because she didn't want him to put her down when he got there. But he didn't. He juggled her and opened the gate, still with her in his arms. Then he was through the front door, clicked his tongue when the door opened without being unlocked, muttering as he went on about lack of security, and then he was standing in the lounge room, looking at the stairs.

'Your room upstairs?'

She nodded. 'I'll walk.'

'I don't think so. You've done enough exercise this morning. I've always wanted to see if I could carry a woman upstairs. We'll give it a go.'

He accomplished the feat with remarkable ease and Tilly couldn't help being impressed. No one had ever carried her like this before.

He paused on the landing only slightly out of breath. Even that was endearing. 'Which is your room?'

She nodded towards the darkest one, painted a deep purple, with beads and crystals in the window. He sat her down on the bed with a quick glance around. 'Let me guess. Purple is the midwives' colour?'

She nodded and he looked into her face and seemed reassured she wasn't going to faint.

He dropped a kiss on her lips that warmed her more than anything since she'd got out of the water and she turned her face to kiss him back. Life was pretty darned precious and the idea of feeling Marcus's arms around her made the demons go away. He pulled back after a longer kiss.

'I'll run the shower.'

Tilly watched him go. Still dazed by the warmth she hadn't expected from him. Maybe he'd got a fright when she'd been in danger? Maybe he was normally a warm and fuzzy person. Yeah, right. Sometimes. She reminded herself she'd gone to great pains to avoid him but that didn't include being rescued from shark-infested waters by a man who up until a couple of weeks ago had hated the water.

And now here he was, making sure she was all right. Running her shower. He certainly revelled in organis-ing people. It was nice but he must think she was the dottiest idiot out, getting caught in a rip in the middle of a shark alert.

She glanced around her room, glad there were no undies on the floor for once to embarrass her. She doubted he'd be so lucky in a bathroom shared by four girls. The thought made her smile and she stood up to get dry clothes. The room swam and she sat down again just as he returned.

'You really are faint.'

She blushed, horrified he'd considered she was put-ting it on. 'I wasn't pretending just to get carried.'

'I didn't mind,' he said softly, and she shot a look at him. The expression on his face confused her. He didn't seem to think she was stupid. He looked like he really did care that she'd had a fright and there was tenderness in his face that made tears itch behind her eyes. He shouldn't look at her like that. What was a girl to think?

'Do you want me to go?'

That was the last thing she wanted. 'Maybe?'

He shook his head and his grin grew wider. 'That wasn't very convincing.' He reached out his hand. 'See if you can stand and if you're okay have a quick shower and get some dry clothes on.' He glanced at her bikini and murmured to himself, 'Not that I'm complaining.'

She pretended not to hear but it was heady to know he was aware of her, physically anyway, as she straightened up carefully. This time she didn't go woozy and her head felt clearer. She'd feel even more normal if the sexual awareness that was growing between them wasn't pulsing like the beat of a drum in her ears. But what did she expect, sitting in her bedroom in her bikini with this man?

Goodness knew what she'd have to do to get him back here ever again, especially if he found out she'd fallen in love with him. Life was too precious. Especially after this morning.

The thought must have crossed her face because he smiled teasingly and turned away. 'Maybe I'll check the shower's cold.'

Please, don't go. She didn't say it out loud but she was darned sure it was in her face. 'Marcus?' He turned back to face her. 'Don't suppose you could stay and hold me for a bit?'

'I'd love to.' He smiled. 'But a gentleman shouldn't take advantage of your weakened state.'

She raised her brows and met his eyes. 'My state's not that weak. It's just a cuddle.'

He patted his damp shirt. 'I'm too damp to sit on your bed.' He reached down for her hand. 'But come up here.' He stood her up, gathered her into his chest, and stroked her hair. 'My poor Matilda. It's been a big morning for you.'

She shivered from the coolness of his shirt, from residual fear and from the idea of losing herself just once in his arms. She couldn't make him love her when he didn't but she could just pretend. 'It could have been my last if you hadn't been there.' She knew it wouldn't mean the same for him but she knew she needed to stay in his arms. Tilly deliberately closed her mind to the reasons she shouldn't ask him to stay with her.

He shook his head and hugged her as if he couldn't help himself then dropped a kiss on her hair. 'The guys in the rubber ducky were coming soon.'

Even with his arms around her she couldn't stop the shaking that had started again. 'Did you know I'd bitten my lip and was terrified the shark was going to smell the blood?' She felt a shiver go through him.

Marcus went cold at the thought and pulled her closer. A sudden dousing of fear ran down his chest. He felt cold, in desperate need of the heat of Matilda. 'Baby. No wonder you were white.' He couldn't imagine the horror if the sharks had sensed the blood. He kissed her lips, and they were cold, too, too cold, and her cheek and her jaw and her throat had such softness of skin it reminded him how vulnerable she was. How terrifyingly easy it would be for her to be gone from his life for ever. He shuddered and this time when he kissed her he showed her he couldn't imagine the horror without her in his arms.

She kissed him back with the same hunger and he slid his hands right down her sides and cupped her buttocks. When he lifted her in his arms she was level with his face, and he murmured, 'Bad sharks,' against her lips. 'Bad, bad sharks.'

He slid her down his body until her feet were on the floor again, a long slide of skin and muscle and unusual prominences she couldn't miss when they both had so little on.

'I'm afraid that's what you do to me,' he said.

'I'm not afraid of you,' she said with a smile, and she watched his eyes grow darker. Not ward eyes, clear and determined, not out-of-work eyes, smiling and fun, but bedroom eyes—deepest, darkest blue. Ones she hadn't seen since that kiss in the kitchen. Eyes that ran over her, possessively, and lit smouldering spot fires everywhere they touched. She'd dreamed he'd look at her like that and it couldn't be wrong if it felt so good.

Such heat and promise and delicious danger lived in those eyes. Her hands slid up his chest, lingeringly, savouring the taut muscles and banded strength, whipcord and curvature she remembered from their lessons, memories stamped in her brain. Dreams that slept with her at night. Why shouldn't she ask for what she wanted? 'If you lifted your arms up I could get that nasty damp shirt off and we could lie on my bed.'

'I could do that.' Back went his strong hands to drag up her sides, skimming her hips and her waist and the outside of her breasts so that she sucked her breath in at the possessiveness he allowed himself with a wicked smile. Then his fingers drifted up her neck, cupped her cheeks and finally lifted strands of her hair until he stood, tall and straight with his hands above his head, daring her to undress him.

The edge of his damp T-shirt scrunched and bunched as she hauled it slowly over his wide chest and finally over his head until it was behind them on the floor. With those eyes on her he reached back with one long arm, shut the door of the room and they were locked in together.

His beautiful bare chest was right in front of her nose, tempting her to flatten her body against him. Teasingly, she resisted, enjoying the fact that she would soon be hard against him, knowing he was impatiently waiting for the same.

'I thought you midwives were really into skin to skin,' he said, as deft fingers undid the bow at the back tie of her bikini and he drew the tiny triangles of fabric over her head until her breasts bounced free and tantalisingly in front of him. He sighed.

'You are...' He enunciated slowly and reverently and there was no humour in his face now, just wonder. 'The most beautiful, sexy woman I have ever seen.'

Then he gathered her into him, bare against his skin, and they both sighed at the sensation until his mouth came down and captured her lips in a kiss that flooded her body with heat.

When he finally lifted his head, he whispered, 'Is that warmer?'

'Much,' she mumbled, and reached up to draw his head back to hers until they were lost again in a kiss.

Much later, when Marcus surfaced, he glanced at his watch and groaned. He kissed her again and rolled to the edge of the bed. He had to go but he so didn't want to. He couldn't believe what had just happened. And didn't want to think about the changes this would mean between them, but for once ramifications could worry about themselves.

'Matilda, my love, I'm so sorry, but I have to go, and if I don't get up now I may not get up at all.' He dropped another kiss on her nose with mock ferocity.

'The next time you want to tempt sharks and pre-cipitate fabulous mornings in bed, can you please give me more notice and I'll take the day off?' He kissed her again, because he loved the fact that she seemed to be still drifting around the ceiling in a post-coital daydream.

'Hmm. I'll try.' She purred like a sleepy cat.

He stood up with a smile. 'Call out if you need me. I'll make us some breakfast and meet you downstairs.' As soon as he'd seen she'd eaten he'd hit the road. He was late already.

Tilly heard Marcus go down the stairs and she opened her eyes. Well, so much for keeping a distance.

She buried her nose in the pillow that still held the indent from his head. But she wouldn't regret this. She hoped.

When Tilly reappeared in her sundress Marcus set the table with slow precision, or he'd have pulled her back into his arms and never left. 'You realise that dress makes me want to slip those thin little straps off your edible shoulders, but I can't or I'll never go.'

She blushed and looked away to the table he'd set and hurriedly picked up her juice.

The toast popped up, and he draped a tea towel across his arm as he bowed over her. 'Would madam like some eggs?'

He watched her eyebrows arch and smiled. It seemed madam would. She nodded and said, 'Good grief. Can you cook as well?'

'I'll have you know I was the favourite chef during my uni years. I worked every morning for a breakfast café in the city.'

She'd probably been in junior high school and he'd bet she was cute.

'I can't cook,' Tilly admitted. 'But I'm great at cleaning up the kitchen after someone else has.'

He kissed his fingertips. 'Then we're perfectly matched.'

Tilly looked down at her fruit and he wasn't sure why she did that. Something had changed.

'So how do you like your eggs?'

'Actually, I'll just have the toast,' she said, but she still didn't meet his eyes.

'What did I say?' He dropped into the chair beside her. 'You okay? It's been a big morning.'

Her smile may have been a little forced but he'd give her full marks for trying. 'I'm fine. Thank you. It's been an amazing morning.'

He leaned over and rubbed her shoulder blades. 'We'll talk about that when we have more time. But, seriously, will you be okay here on your own?'

She leaned back into his hands. 'Why? Don't you have somewhere to go?'

He glanced at his watch. 'Soon. But I want to make sure you're okay.'

'I'm okay. And I'll just have the toast, thanks.'

When Marcus had left, Tilly sank down on the chair in the kitchen and put her head in her hands. What if he dropped her now like the others had? She couldn't believe she'd done it. Not the sex, though that had been a decision fraught with danger and hadn't helped her dilemma, but actually done what she'd said she wouldn't. She'd fallen in love with him.

Completely, utterly, besottedly in love with Marcus Bennett, and in such a way that she knew any previous love she'd thought she'd felt was nothing. That puppy infatuation couldn't rip her into pieces like this emotion could. What if he never came to care for her like she cared? She was doomed.

The man she'd promised blithely she didn't want to be anything but friends with now filled her mind.

Marcus drove into the city and as he shifted between the lanes he thought about Tilly and how explosive and amazing the passion between them had been. Crazy and totally unexpected and almost out of control but fed by the danger she'd faced this morning.

He'd never been so scared for another person in his life and he didn't know how he'd come to be so dependent on her wellbeing. Obviously he was infatuated with her. If it was infatuation and not something much more shattering. He'd always promised himself he'd leave his main focus on work and the intrusion of Tilly into his thoughts was becoming a serious distraction.

But it seemed his ability to be focussed and driven to achieve his goals could be split with a portion diverted and directed towards Tilly and the idea of pursuing her had sprouted in his subconscious. Not a lot he could do about it.

He remembered her saying she was not willing to risk her heart for a few years. Well, at least they had time. Maybe a few weeks was a little quick to capture her full attention but after today he had a whole new armoury of weapons.

He pulled up at the traffic lights and glanced in the rear-view mirror. The bloke in the mirror was smiling like a goof. Let's see what he can do then. Maybe he could start with her passions.

Over the next few days, in every spare moment, Marcus read everything he could find on water birth, home-birth statistics, current trends in birthing, and the latest government initiatives for mothers and babies. A lot of it he knew, some of it he'd had no idea about, and some of it, he had to admit, he'd got the wrong impression about.

'So with a water birth, what's your understanding of why a baby doesn't breathe?' They were sitting on the headland, watching the waves, as the light faded behind them and Marcus had his arm around her.

Several blocks of sutured foam were in a little canvas bag beside them. They'd spent half an hour sewing pretend wound repairs and Tilly was feeling quietly confident she could do a good job. But tomorrow they'd try the steak.

Marcus's arm felt warm and solid, and very dear, and she was starting to wonder if the most stupid thing she'd ever done had been to sleep with him. Because it had changed the way she was aware of him, changed the way all her senses stood up and waved when he was near, nudged her whole body into his space so that it was natural that they touch a lot of the time now.

Except when they were at work. Thank goodness she could block him out at work.

Tilly saw a fish skim through a wall of water and thought about his question. 'Are you saying you don't know or you've been reading up and you want to see what my version is?'

'Tilly, you're beginning to understand me too well.' He glanced at her with a knowing smile. 'I may have been reading a little.'

She smiled. 'I have no idea when you'd get the time.'

'Look who's talking. You swim, teach Nippers, ren-ovate houses and do rallies in your spare moments.

There's always a minute to learn something, isn't there? So what can you teach me about this?'

So he wanted to learn from her? She didn't quite believe she could teach him anything if he'd been reading. But you never knew. 'I'm quite good at explaining water birth.' She was, actually. 'I've had enough practice over the years with my mother's clients.'

He didn't say anything and she went on with a teasing glint in her eye. 'Because it's the most common reason people choose to birth at home when the hospital won't allow it?'

She waited.

'I hear you,' he said mildly, and she had to be content with that. They were both happy their unfurling relationship didn't spill over at work.

'The theory is that before birth babies are surrounded by fluid so babies seem to find birth in water effortless. It must be less traumatic for them to be born into the warm environment they're used to rather than cold air and light and other people apart from their parents touching them.

'Assuming there's not a torch in their eyes and somebody grabbing at their head,' he added sagely, and she had to smile.

'That's true. That's one of the reasons an experienced birth assistant is needed, yes.'

'And they don't breathe because…?' They way he kept looking at her and smiling made it hard to concentrate.

'At birth babies are stimulated to breathe by exposure

to air when it hits their face. Trigeminal response. The air hitting the triangle of skin around the mouth and nose.'

'And they breathe when we stimulate them,' Marcus added. 'Rubbing them over with a towel?'

She nodded. 'Which is why babies stay completely submerged in a water birth and aren't over-handled until their head breaks the surface.'

'I'd get nervous if a baby was taking a long time to crown.'

'They don't need to breathe for those first moments. The placenta is still giving them the oxygen, like it does in a normal land birth. We take them out before the placenta comes away.'

'And once they do reach air, they don't go under again.'

'Absolutely not. It's why we don't stimulate them with lots of handling while they're birthing under water. Basically that's the only slight risk and a non-stressed baby would not have the stimulation to breathe.'

'So stressed babies may gasp underwater at birth. I read that.'

'In theory. But to balance that risk there's the inherent dive reflex of babies.'

'I needed a dive reflex to make me go in the water.'

'You've got one now. I saw you.'

'Tell me about the dive reflex babies have.'

'I know you know this.'

'Yeah, but I love the way you explain things.'

'Do you?'

'Yes, Miss Fishing-for-a-compliment.'

Well, I love all of you. In fact, I'm in love with you. But she couldn't say that. He'd run a mile. She dragged her thoughts back to the question. At least the topic absorbed her.

He watched her face. The passion, excitement there, absolute certainty that this was a fabulous way for a baby to enter the world and how she wanted him to see that. He wasn't so sure about it being any better than normal but maybe it wasn't rocket science.

'Well, if water reaches the chemo receptors on a baby's tongue, it doesn't breathe like an adult might. Instead, it swallows and slows down its heart rate and goes into a protective state.'

He was watching her with that strange expression on his face again. She wound down. 'So a baby has this warm transition from warm water to head up on mum's chest and lovely skin to skin with nobody getting cold. Even the air is humidified from the steam in the room for its newly breathing lungs, no bright lights for unaccustomed eyes, and just the parents' hands.' She looked at him. 'It must be soothing for everybody.'

'You're soothing for everybody.'

Then as they sat looking out over the ocean he told her about his parents and his sister and the scars he'd carried for so long. Scars she'd helped to heal just by him knowing her.

CHAPTER TWELVE

'KEEP Sunday free for me. At your castle. Eight o'clock,' Marcus reminded her. He hoped she wouldn't forget.

He'd put a lot of thought into how he was going to woo Matilda. His wooing had to prove not just to Matilda but also to himself that he could let go of his compulsive desire for control.

He still had major issues with Tilly swimming in the bay with those sharks able to glide in at any time, but Duggie had given him a stern talking to about sensible ocean etiquette and the fact that Tilly was an experienced swimmer.

He had to deal with that. He'd always prefer to run. That paddle out to Tilly hadn't endeared him to the beach and now that he could swim, she could have it.

Then he saw her. Here she comes, Marcus thought as she appeared at the bottom of Hill Street. She had on that little green sundress that reflected in her eyes. His body stirred with delighted recognition as that determined little walk he loved closed the distance between them.

If he'd been a dog his tail would be wagging like mad. He was a basket case and he'd never thought he'd be a loon like this over a gorgeous little midwife who drove him insane with lust and laughter. It was as if he'd taken off dark glasses he'd worn all his life. Suddenly, when Tilly was around, the world was a sunnier place and he could never thank her enough.

He saw she had his favourite earrings on and they brushed against her neck. Delightful memories. His smile widened. Earrings for breakfast was a good sign she had an inkling this was special.

He'd tried to make it so. He'd called on all his experience from his coffee-shop days, the way the waitresses had tarted up the restaurant for special occasions, added touches that the women patrons had crooned over.

That's what he wanted for Tilly. Crooning. One day he'd really sing to her. Once he'd learnt the words to the right song. He couldn't help his smile becoming a grin.

When Tilly walked down to the rotunda at the park she had a strange feeling of anticipation. Everything was fraught with danger now that she'd admitted to herself she loved Marcus.

Everything had changed since they'd made love. He was so considerate, seemed always to be aware of her, and the attention was intoxicating. But she was definitely scared that it would all end. She'd got it wrong before and wasn't keen to second-guess his intentions in case she made the same mistake. What they had at the moment was pretty darned incredible and she should be satisfied with that.

She drew a deep breath and the salty air grounded her because life was amazing. To her left two kids kicked a ball, the drone of a plane hummed in the background, and the waves pounded on the beach in the way they had for aeons. The air was still and warm and a few seagulls fought over a dropped crust from a child's sandwich as she walked the last few feet across the park.

Would she be happy with the crumbs if that was all Marcus had? She didn't know.

Her heart skittered and then he was in front of her. Marcus. Waiting beside her castle. Her lovely man. Her knight who cared deeply for others, who wanted nothing more than safe mothers and babies in a world that bred fear, who'd learnt to listen to her perception of trust in a woman's natural ability. It hadn't been easy for him. And she'd learnt to listen. Breathe, even a little, before exploding. She smiled to herself. Which was a good thing.

He was smiling at her and she couldn't take her eyes off him. Such a hunk, it wasn't fair, she just wanted to wrap her arms around him and feel safe and cherished in the way only he seemed able to make her feel.

He held out his hand and the sense of homecoming just by placing her fingers in his melted her heart.

'Your castle awaits.' Magic seemed to shimmer in the air between them and she saw two chairs and a table had been shifted from the take-away stall so they could sit down. He'd commandeered the whole thing. Typical, arrogant male. She loved it. And him.

Then she saw that with the ocean as backdrop, each pole of the wrought-iron rotunda had a flower pot with a profusion of white daisies that waved gaily at Tilly in the salty breeze as she walked up the stairs. It looked pretty and romantic, and crazily extravagant.

Even a red-hatted gnome in the middle looked happy. She blushed but it was very cool. 'When did you do this?'

The plane droned and he nodded sagely. 'I have elves who help me.'

'Why are you doing this?'

'Today is our one-month-since-we-met anniversary.'

'One month. It feels like a year.'

He smiled. 'When I first met you, to my shame, I worried that people would talk about us at the hospital.'

She'd known that but it hadn't worried her. Apparently it had worried him. 'I can understand that. You'd just taken over a high-profile position.'

One of the elves, who looked suspiciously like the waiter from the Beachside Bistro, carried a platter of melons and strawberries and a tub of creamy cinnamon yoghurt across to them.

'For your princess,' the waiter said with a flourish, and his face was spit with a romantic's pleasure. '*L'amore,*' he sang cheekily as he went away.

Marcus reached down into an esky she only then realised was beside his chair and he produced a bottle of sparkling non-alcoholic wine in honour of the park's

no-alcohol policy, and two really pretty fluted but un-
deniably plastic glasses. He poured carefully, topped
up with orange juice, placed one flute in front of her
and then one in front of himself.

'A toast?'

'To what?' She was bemused. Kept looking at the
daisies, and the gnome and the tablecloth, and the subdued mischievousness that emanated from Marcus. Another different Marcus she hadn't met.

'A lack of sea breeze for half an hour at least. Which
is why we're here in the morning and not the afternoon.'

She frowned. 'Because?'

'He needs to finish the sentence.' He grimaced.
'There's absolutely nothing I can do if the wind springs
up.' He frowned and then smiled. 'You will be pleased
to know I have actually given up control of something.'

Even more confusing. 'Who does? What wind?'

Marcus looked at her and smiled and reached out
with those beautiful long fingers and gathered her hand
in his again. With his other hand he pointed to the sky
over the blue ocean.

'I LOVE YOU TILL…' The plane came around for
the last letter and already the 'I' was starting to bloom
out into a thicker white letter. Then it was done. 'Y.' 'I
LOVE YOU TILLY.'

Tilly couldn't believe this was happening, in the
park, on a Sunday, with dozens of people watching.
Mr Unobtrusive telling the world. Her name in the blue
sky. A declaration for the whole of Sydney to see.

People were pointing to the words in the sky from the beach. Some of them were looking at her.

She could feel a tide of delighted pink staining her cheeks and then she forgot the other people. Could only see Marcus. Could only feel his strength and warmth and love as he took her hand and looked into her face.

'I know this is kind of sudden but it came to me in a flash. Matilda McPherson, I need to tell you something. Loudly. Which isn't my style, so I thought you might like this—and maybe even believe me.'

He paused and glanced at the sky as if for inspiration. 'I love you.' He read it out slowly. And grinned sheepishly—looking as if he couldn't believe he'd arranged that himself. 'You bowled me over on the first day. Literally.' They both looked at the gnome and smiled. 'And you've stolen a little more of my heart every time we've met. And now—you have it all.'

He drew a breath. 'When you were out in the water with that shark alarm I'd never been so scared in my life. I can't lose you.'

Tilly stared out from her princess tower to the sky above and the words that were there for all the world to see—even if only briefly. Fluffy white stretched out letters that were already floating out to sea, stretching into elongated wisps of vapour, dissipating into the sky but written on her memory for ever. She hoped he'd arranged one of his elves to photograph that before it was gone. Knowing him, he would have. She stopped worrying about it.

She sniffed back the tears, the thickness in her throat,

the explosion of heat in her heart. 'Marcus, what can I say after that magnificent declaration? I'm thinking I might even believe you.'

They both stood up, and she wasn't sure how it happened but suddenly she was in his arms, and in the distance she could hear people clapping.

He looked down at her quizzically, almost sternly, like the Dr Bennett she knew too well. 'You could say something else.'

She laughed and hugged him fiercely. 'I love you, too, Marcus. Of course I love you.'

Marcus hugged her back. This place would always be special to him because it had given him Tilly. Already he was plotting what he could do to surprise her when he asked her to marry him. No doubt his aunt and her friends would want to sing at their wedding.

Marcus smiled. He was definitely going to learn to sing, too.

* * * * *

SEPTEMBER 2011
HARDBACK TITLES

ROMANCE

The Kanellis Scandal	Michelle Reid
Monarch of the Sands	Sharon Kendrick
One Night in the Orient	Robyn Donald
His Poor Little Rich Girl	Melanie Milburne
The Sultan's Choice	Abby Green
The Return of the Stranger	Kate Walker
Girl in the Bedouin Tent	Annie West
Once Touched, Never Forgotten	Natasha Tate
Nice Girls Finish Last	Natalie Anderson
The Italian Next Door...	Anna Cleary
From Daredevil to Devoted Daddy	Barbara McMahon
Little Cowgirl Needs a Mum	Patricia Thayer
To Wed a Rancher	Myrna Mackenzie
Once Upon a Time in Tarrula	Jennie Adams
The Secret Princess	Jessica Hart
Blind Date Rivals	Nina Harrington
Cort Mason – Dr Delectable	Carol Marinelli
Survival Guide to Dating Your Boss	Fiona McArthur

HISTORICAL

The Lady Gambles	Carole Mortimer
Lady Rosabella's Ruse	Ann Lethbridge
The Viscount's Scandalous Return	Anne Ashley
The Viking's Touch	Joanna Fulford

MEDICAL ROMANCE™

Return of the Maverick	Sue MacKay
It Started with a Pregnancy	Scarlet Wilson
Italian Doctor, No Strings Attached	Kate Hardy
Miracle Times Two	Josie Metcalfe

0811 Gen Std L

SEPTEMBER 2011
LARGE PRINT TITLES

ROMANCE

Too Proud to be Bought	Sharon Kendrick
A Dark Sicilian Secret	Jane Porter
Prince of Scandal	Annie West
The Beautiful Widow	Helen Brooks
Rancher's Twins: Mum Needed	Barbara Hannay
The Baby Project	Susan Meier
Second Chance Baby	Susan Meier
Her Moment in the Spotlight	Nina Harrington

HISTORICAL

More Than a Mistress	Ann Lethbridge
The Return of Lord Conistone	Lucy Ashford
Sir Ashley's Mettlesome Match	Mary Nichols
The Conqueror's Lady	Terri Brisbin

MEDICAL ROMANCE™

Summer Seaside Wedding	Abigail Gordon
Reunited: A Miracle Marriage	Judy Campbell
The Man with the Locked Away Heart	Melanie Milburne
Socialite...or Nurse in a Million?	Molly Evans
St Piran's: The Brooding Heart Surgeon	Alison Roberts
Playboy Doctor to Doting Dad	Sue MacKay

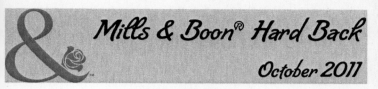

ROMANCE

The Most Coveted Prize	Penny Jordan
The Costarella Conquest	Emma Darcy
The Night that Changed Everything	Anne McAllister
Craving the Forbidden	India Grey
The Lost Wife	Maggie Cox
Heiress Behind the Headlines	Caitlin Crews
Weight of the Crown	Christina Hollis
Innocent in the Ivory Tower	Lucy Ellis
Flirting With Intent	Kelly Hunter
A Moment on the Lips	Kate Hardy
Her Italian Soldier	Rebecca Winters
The Lonesome Rancher	Patricia Thayer
Nikki and the Lone Wolf	Marion Lennox
Mardie and the City Surgeon	Marion Lennox
Bridesmaid Says, 'I Do!'	Barbara Hannay
The Princess Test	Shirley Jump
Breaking Her No-Dates Rule	Emily Forbes
Waking Up With Dr Off-Limits	Amy Andrews

HISTORICAL

The Lady Forfeits	Carole Mortimer
Valiant Soldier, Beautiful Enemy	Diane Gaston
Winning the War Hero's Heart	Mary Nichols
Hostage Bride	Anne Herries

MEDICAL ROMANCE™

Tempted by Dr Daisy	Caroline Anderson
The Fiancée He Can't Forget	Caroline Anderson
A Cotswold Christmas Bride	Joanna Neil
All She Wants For Christmas	Annie Claydon

GEN STD HB

Mills & Boon® Large Print
October 2011

ROMANCE

Passion and the Prince	Penny Jordan
For Duty's Sake	Lucy Monroe
Alessandro's Prize	Helen Bianchin
Mr and Mischief	Kate Hewitt
Her Desert Prince	Rebecca Winters
The Boss's Surprise Son	Teresa Carpenter
Ordinary Girl in a Tiara	Jessica Hart
Tempted by Trouble	Liz Fielding

HISTORICAL

Secret Life of a Scandalous Debutante	Bronwyn Scott
One Illicit Night	Sophia James
The Governess and the Sheikh	Marguerite Kaye
Pirate's Daughter, Rebel Wife	June Francis

MEDICAL ROMANCE™

Taming Dr Tempest	Meredith Webber
The Doctor and the Debutante	Anne Fraser
The Honourable Maverick	Alison Roberts
The Unsung Hero	Alison Roberts
St Piran's: The Fireman and Nurse Loveday	Kate Hardy
From Brooding Boss to Adoring Dad	Dianne Drake